SAYING YES TO THE MILLIONAIRE

SAYING YES TO THE MILLIONAIRE

BY

FIONA HARPER

First published in Great Britain 2008
Large Print edition 2008
Harlequin Mills & Boon Limited,
Eton House, 18-24 Paradise Road,
Richmond, Surrey TW9 1SR

ISBN: 978 0 263 20088 1

Set in Times Roman 16½ on 18¼ pt.
16-1008-56738

Printed and bound in Great Britain
by Antony Rowe Ltd, Chippenham, Wiltshire

For Kirsteen, my naughty little sister,
who has travelled the world and bungee-jumped
while I've just sat at home and daydreamed about it.

CHAPTER ONE

'NO, I CAN'T. I don't think I can do this!'

Solid ground was a distant memory. Fern glanced down past her feet and a tidal wave of nausea crashed in her stomach. The Thames glittered in the June sun and London politely carried on about its business one hundred and fifty feet below her. Someone behind her muttered, 'Is she going to jump or not?'

Not. Definitely not. Surely, if God had meant us to do this we'd have been born with lengths of elastic attached to our feet.

She gulped. Every muscle in her body had tightened itself into a dozen knots. She closed her eyes, but that just made things worse. The darkness magnified the dull roar of the traffic and the flap of the bungee cord as it swung in the faint breeze. Her body swayed.

No. She was not going to do this.

Her eyes snapped open and she twisted her

head, opening her mouth to tell them it had all been a horrible mistake. But, before the sounds emerged from the back of her throat, a warm pair of hands steadied her on either side of her waist.

'She's all right. Aren't you, Fern?'

Fern shook her head, but the squeak that finally made it out of her mouth sounded an awful lot like *yes*.

She caught a faint hint of aftershave as he moved closer, felt his breath as it tickled the fine tendrils of hair that had worked their way out of her ponytail and now curled in front of her ears.

'You can do this.' The voice sounded so warm and reassuring. 'You know that, don't you?'

For a second, Fern almost forgot where she was, high on a crane on the banks of the Thames. Almost forgot the crowd of onlookers and charity event organisers looking up at her from the hard concrete below. She recognised that voice!

Josh was here.

And he was right behind her, whispering words of encouragement into her ear. Her pulse didn't know whether to speed up, slow down or stop altogether. But, bizarrely, she felt safe with him there, so close she could feel the beat of his heart against her back.

'Yes,' she whispered. This time, she half-believed her answer.

'So…I'm going to count to three, and when I say *go*, you just allow yourself to fall.'

He had the most delicious voice. It seemed to curl and roll inside her ears. She got carried away just listening to the sounds, the individual syllables, forgetting the meaning of the words. And then suddenly she realised he was saying *three*.

'But I—'

He didn't shout; he said the next word so gently it was almost as if he'd just breathed out. 'Go.'

And then she was falling, falling—the breath sucked so hard from her body that she couldn't even scream.

Three days earlier…

'No, thank you.' Fern shook her head once, firmly, hoping Lisette would get the message. She should have known better. Her friend waved something slimy-looking on a fork in front of her face, so close she was going cross-eyed trying to focus on it.

'Go on! Try it.'

'Really, Lisette. No. I don't like seafood.'

'It's squid. Hardly tastes of anything.' The fork swayed in a hypnotising motion. 'We've been coming to Giovanni's once a month for the past year and each time you order exactly the same.'

Fern fended the squid-loaded cutlery off with her hand. 'I like Pasta Neapolitana. It's my favourite.'

Lisette threw her fork down on her plate. 'It's boring, that's what it is.'

'It's nice. And I don't run the risk of food poisoning if it hasn't been cooked or stored properly.'

'Spoken like a true Health and Safety specialist.'

Fern stabbed a pasta bow with her fork, put it in her mouth and chewed, all the time staring defiantly at her friend. Lisette was always poking fun at her job. She swallowed her mouthful and took a sip of wine. Not everybody could have an outlandish job like Lisette's. And besides, her job might seem routine, but she helped people, kept them safe.

'Talking of jobs, what are you up to next week?'

Lisette popped the squid in her mouth and swallowed, wearing a playful smile as she gulped it down. 'Guess.'

Fern rolled her eyes. Lisette's main work was being a professional 'extra'. She could end up sitting in a pub in one of the weekly soaps or dressed up in tin-foil for a sci-fi series. Variety might be the spice of life, but Fern couldn't understand how Lisette tolerated a job with sporadic work, long hours and four o'clock in the morning starts.

'Lis, I haven't got a clue. Why don't you just tell me?'

'I've got a spot on a new police drama. Next week my uniform will be fishnets, high heels and a wicked glint in my eye.'

A small crease appeared between Fern's brows. 'Since when did police officers wear fishnets?'

Lisette grinned at her. 'Come on, can you really picture me in big clumpy heels and a neat white shirt? I'm going to be "Hooker Number Three". Cool, huh?'

Fern nodded, perhaps a little too hard. Lisette gave her a knowing smile.

'I'm sorry, Lis. I'm really pleased you've got the work but…'

'Standing up in front of a room full of people and being outrageous is just not your cup of tea. I know. Horses for courses, and all that. I'd die of boredom being an insurance investigator.'

'Risk analyst,' Fern reminded her, although she didn't know why she bothered. Lisette always got her job title wrong. You just had to mention the word 'insurance' or 'office' and Lis's eyes glazed over.

'Yeah, yeah. I remember.'

They returned their attention to their food. Lisette speared a mussel and paused before she put the fork into her mouth. 'If not squid, how about one of these?'

Fern sighed. 'No.'

'D'you know,' Lis said, still munching the dollop of yuckiness, 'I think I hear you say that word more than any other in your vocabulary.'

'No, you don't.'

Lisette stabbed the air with her fork in a *got you* kind of manner. Fern looked at her plate and decided she couldn't be bothered with the rest.

'See? You're bored with that already. What you need is a bit more excitement in your life.'

Oh, yeah. Here we go.

Lisette saw it as her mission in life to liven up her poor, deprived friend. Over the years she'd dragged her along to all sorts of strange activities: kickboxing, paragliding, weird yoga classes where you were supposed to fold yourself up like a pretzel…And when those attempts had failed it had got even worse. Next she'd started trying to find exciting men for Fern to date. After an evening with Brad the Formula One driver, she'd been scared of getting in a car for a week.

'No, I do not.'

Lis's mouth stretched into a thin, wide smile. 'There's that word again. You just can't help yourself, can you?'

'*Yes*. I can.' Now it was her turn to wear the wide smile.

Lisette shovelled more pasta into her mouth and as she chewed she stared thoughtfully at the ceiling. When she'd finished she sat back in her chair and folded her arms. 'I reckon if you had to go a week without saying *no*, you'd shrivel up and die.'

'Now you're just being ridiculous.'

'Am I? Okay, let's see just how ridiculous my theory is.'

Fern really should have listened to her instinct to get up and sprint out of the restaurant door at that point but she was too intrigued to miss out on the last part of her character assassination.

Lisette nodded to herself and then looked Fern square in the eye. 'I challenge you to say *yes* to every question you are asked for one whole week.'

Fern laughed so hard that a couple of other diners turned round to stare at her and she clapped a hand over her mouth. 'And why on earth would I accept a challenge like that?'

A glint appeared in Lisette's eye. Fern's stomach dropped. When Lis thought on the hop like this, there was normally trouble to follow. Her brain was likely to kangaroo off in all sorts of directions and come up with some really stupid ideas.

'Because I will donate five hundred pounds to your Leukaemia Research thingy if you do it.'

That was below the belt. How was she going to refuse an offer like that? The cancer research charity she championed desperately needed more funds for vital research—research into treatments that might have saved Ryan's life all those years ago, if they'd been available. The charity was asking its volunteer fundraisers to try and raise one hundred thousand pounds. She'd been on countless fun runs, had sponsored this-and-thats, all to hike the total up—and they were so close now. Five thousand pounds to go. What Lisette was offering was a tenth of that. More than she could ever hope to raise by herself in one week.

'You're insane.'

'Quite possibly. But I'd quite happily hand over the cash if I got to see you take a few chances, live life a little. You're stuck in a rut, darling.'

No, she wasn't! She opened her mouth to tell Lisette so, but then realised she'd just be using *that* word again and it would only encourage her.

'Perhaps I like my rut.'

Lisette leaned back to let the waiter clear their plates. 'That, my dear Fern, is the heart of the problem. You need to break out of it now, before you hit middle age and get stuck in it for ever.'

If her insides hadn't been churning, the dramatic look on Lisette's face would have made her want to laugh. She took a deep breath. Her friend might be letting her imagination run away with her, but she still had some weapons of her own. Logic. Good sense. Sanity, even.

'You haven't thought this through at all. I couldn't possibly say yes to every question somebody asked me in a week. What if somebody asked me if I wanted to rob a bank, or set myself on fire?'

'Yes, complete strangers always wander up to you in London and ask you to join them in a spot of light burglary.'

Fern looked heavenwards and pushed her plate even further away from her. It was invading her personal space, making her feel uncomfortable. 'You're over-dramatising again. You know what I'm talking about. Someone could ask me to look the other way while they stole something or ask me to do something risky. I know the rest of the world might see London as being so very proper and a little bit stuffy but, let's face it, there are nutters roaming the streets of this city.'

Lisette should know. She'd dated half of them.

'You're right.' Lisette dug in her handbag for a pen and started doodling on a napkin. Really not a good idea as this was the sort of establishment that didn't use paper napkins but linen ones. 'We need some ground rules.'

'*We* don't need any rules at all. I'm not doing it.'

Lisette carried on scribbling. 'Okay, there are some get out clauses. Nothing illegal. Nothing truly dangerous.'

'Nothing immoral.' Why was she joining in? This wasn't going to go anywhere.

Lisette looked up at that point. 'Nothing immoral? Pity. You're cancelling out a whole lot of fun that way.'

'It might sound fun to you, but I'm certainly not

going to say yes if some guy walks up to me and asks me to…you know.'

'Like I said, cancelling out a whole lot of fun, but I'll concede. You're allowed to say no if it's something truly against your conscience.'

'Gee, thanks.' A cheeky smile spread across her lips and lifted her cheeks. 'How are you going to keep a check on me? You can't follow me round all week. What if I cheat?'

Lisette went so still for a second that Fern thought her heart must have stopped, and then she laughed so loudly that the man behind Fern turned round again and glared at her. Fern gave him an it-wasn't-me-this-time shrug and turned back to face Lisette, who was wiping her eyes. There was a smudge of mascara on Lis's cheek. She decided not to tell her about it.

'Nah. Don't think so, my little Fern. Even if you were tempted, you'd cave in when I handed you the cheque and you'd confess all, wouldn't you?'

'No!' What kind of sap did her flatmate think she was? But, then again…She buried her head in her hands, her shoulder-length blonde hair swinging forward to hide her face. 'Oh, all right. Yes, I would.'

'If there's one person in this crazy world who

is guaranteed to do the right thing, the sensible thing, it's you.'

Fern picked up the dessert menu and stared at it. 'And that's exactly why I'm not going to take any part in your crazy scheme.'

'Really? I mean, really?' Lisette dipped the menu down with the tip of one of her fingers so she could look into Fern's eyes. 'Think of it as another sponsored event. I'm sponsoring you to prise yourself from your rut for one week. Just one week. You can do that, can't you? For charity?' She batted her eyelids, a completely ridiculous gesture, but somehow it always worked on Fern.

Drat that woman! After living with her for three years, she knew exactly where Fern's weak points were. And raising money to prevent any more children going through the pain and sickness that her brother had endured before his death, to stop any more families being left with a large gaping hole that could never be filled, was something she couldn't walk away from.

'I can walk away at any time?'

Lisette shrugged. 'You can. But you won't get the money. It'll be up to you.'

Fern picked up a wineglass and sloshed back the rest of the contents. 'Okay. Yes. I'll do it.' For

Ryan. Here's to you, big brother, she thought as she swallowed the Chardonnay.

Lisette clapped her hands and rubbed them together with glee. 'I'm going to make sure you have the most exciting week of your life!'

Fern reached for the wine bottle and poured herself another glass. That was exactly what she'd been afraid of.

'Sorry, Callum. You're going to have to take the New York meeting on your own.' Josh stuck his head through the doorway into the living room and spotted his father dozing on the sofa with the paper over his face. He nudged the door closed and lowered his voice. 'My dad is getting better—slowly—but I'm going to stick around for at least another fortnight.'

While his business partner lamented that he was going to miss a vital appointment with the head of an exclusive hotel chain, Josh wandered from the hallway into the kitchen and stared out of the window into the garden. Callum would cope fine without him; he was such a worrier. Personally, Josh was more disappointed at abandoning the trip he'd had planned *after* New York—a planned visit to one of his pet projects.

Recently One Life Travel had opened a non-profit making arm that organised charity expeditions. Want to walk the Great Wall of China to help save the whales? Or canoe up the Amazon to raise funds to fight heart disease? Then the new One Life Expeditions was the place to go.

The Amazon. He sighed. He'd been really looking forward to a spot of canoeing. He'd planned to join one of the latest expeditions to personally see if the company was getting it right—if the guides were good, the equipment safe, the staff knowledgeable.

This hands-on personal touch, a rigid policy of road-testing absolutely everything, was why what had started as a simple website offering good advice and cheap deals for backpackers had mushroomed into an award-winning travel corporation. They were in the business of offering once-in-a-lifetime trips, whether that be cheap flights and even cheaper hostels for the backpackers, or exclusive individually tailored trips with five-star elegance for a more discerning clientele.

He could see his mother kneeling on the lawn, planting petunias. His parents' garden was beautiful, no doubt about that. But it was too…tame. And too small. No chance of running into snakes on the bowling green lawn or piranhas in the fish pond, more's the pity.

'It'll be fine. Take Sara with you,' he told Callum. His PA was so efficient it would almost be as if he were there in person. 'She knows the deal inside out. I'll call you in a week and give you an update.'

He said his goodbyes and left the cordless phone on the kitchen counter. Mum would nag him about that in a minute.

It seemed odd being back in this house, even sleeping in his old bedroom rather than in his own house on the other side of town. Nothing had changed here. Oh, there were different kitchen cabinets and a new three-piece suite, but the atmosphere, the essence of the place was the same. Comforting and stifling all at the same time.

Of course, Mum was delighted to have him here. She hardly let him out of her sight. But maybe that was to be expected. Nowadays he only really made it home for big celebrations, like dad's sixtieth—had that really been six months ago?—and Christmas dinner. Well, most Christmas dinners. Last December he'd been left stranded in Nepal after a trek through the Himalayan foothills, his flight cancelled.

It was good to see his parents again, but he'd

rather it had been under different circumstances. Six weeks ago, he'd got a frantic call from his mother letting him know that his father was undergoing emergency heart surgery. He'd flown straight home. It had been touch and go for a few days, but Dad was pulling through.

He didn't want to think about the ten-hour flight home. It had been the first time in years that he hadn't enjoyed the rush of take-off. All he'd been able to think about was how little he'd seen his parents in the last few months and how awful it would be if…

He shook his head and stepped through the open back door and walked towards his mother, leaving that thought behind in the bright and cheery kitchen. His feet were itchy. He wanted to be here for his father but, at the same time, now that Dad was on the mend he was starting to feel like a spare part.

Mum was now standing on the lawn, hands on hips, surveying her handiwork.

'They look nice, Mum.'

She turned and looked at him, her face screwed up against the bright sunshine. 'Not very exotic, I know, but I like them. It makes the place feel like home.'

Josh smiled back at her and his gaze drifted down the garden. It was a good-sized plot for a semi-detached house of this size, stretching back more than a hundred feet. A big garden, in London suburb terms. It looked lighter, somehow. The bottom of the garden had always seemed so shady in his childhood memories.

And then he realised something was missing.

'Mum? What happened to the old apple tree?'

She wiped her hands on the front of her old gardening jeans and walked over to stand by his side. 'We had some heavy winds this spring. Eighty mile an hour gusts at times.' She shrugged. 'Woke up the next morning to find most of the apple tree in next door's garden.'

He instantly set off walking towards where the apple tree had once been. Only a stump was left. Suddenly he felt angry. That tree had been a huge part of his childhood. He and Ryan, the boy next door and his best friend, had spent more time in its branches during the summer months than they had with their feet on the earth. If he'd known the last time he'd been here that it would be the last time he'd see it, he would have…dunno… said a prayer or something.

He didn't like graveyards. They were way too

permanent. And he hadn't been to visit the small marble headstone in St Mark's churchyard, not even on the day of Ryan's funeral. Instead, he'd come here to the apple tree. He'd climbed up into the highest branches and sat silently with his legs swinging. If only…

If only he'd realised that summer, when he'd been thirteen and Ryan had been fourteen, that it would be their last one together. He would have made sure they finished the tree-house they'd been planning to build in those old branches, not just left it as a few planks nailed in strategic places.

A cold, dark feeling swirled inside his stomach. It threatened to bubble up and overwhelm him. Suddenly his legs were moving and he was striding back towards the house.

His mother, as she always was in his thoughts of her when he was half a world away, was putting the kettle on for a cup of tea. Once back inside the kitchen, he shut the back door, even though the gentle breeze and the warm, buzzing sound of the bees in the lavender below the window would have been pleasant.

'You still miss him, don't you?'

He shrugged with just one shoulder, then

looked at his feet. Mum would scold him for not using the doormat on his way in. He went back and rectified the situation. When he looked up, she was giving him one of those don't-think-you-can-fool-me looks.

What good would it do to tell her that, on one level, he still expected Ryan to barge in through the back door and charm his mother into giving him a slice of her famous Victoria sponge? He looked out of the window into the Chambers's garden next door.

'I haven't seen Fern since I've been back.'

His mother reached into a cupboard and pulled out the teapot. 'Her mother says she's very busy at work.'

He nodded. That was Fern. Dedicated, hard-working, loyal to a fault. 'I hope she's not overdoing it.'

His mother laughed. 'You're as bad as Jim and Helen! The poor girl gets nagged and smothered at every turn. No wonder she moved out.'

Ah, but Mum didn't know about the promise. The day of Ryan's funeral, hidden up in the old apple tree, he'd adopted the girl next door as his honorary little sister and vowed to watch out for her. Oh, he'd teased and tormented her just as

Ryan would have done, but he'd protected her too. To his own cost sometimes.

Mum reached for the tea caddy. 'Don't think much of her flatmate, though. A bit of a wild thing.'

His features hardened. Fern had a flatmate? Male or female?

'Is…is she seeing anyone?'

His mother shook her head. 'Not that I know of. There was someone serious last year. I was sure they were on the verge of settling down but then he upped and disappeared.'

'Am I allowed to find him, then punch him?'

Billowing steam poured from the kettle, matching his mood nicely. A shrill whistle announced it was at boiling point and he automatically turned the gas off. The kitchen was silent again.

'She's not nine any more, you know,' his mother said.

He knew. It was just easier to think of her that way.

'Like I said, you're as bad as her parents. You all want to wrap her up in cotton wool. She puts up with it for their sake, because of Ryan, but mark my words, she's not going to thank you for joining in.'

Nonsense. Fern loved seeing him. He was her favourite honorary big brother.

Mum reached forward and ruffled his hair.

'Mu-um!'

'Not that I could ever pin you down long enough to wrap you up in anything.' She walked over to the back door and opened it, letting the warm sunshine in. 'But I'm scared to death half the time when you're off doing those extreme sports. I can sympathise with the desire to keep your only child safe.'

'I've told you before; I can look after myself.'

Time to change the subject.

'Are you sure you won't let me pay for that holiday, Mum? You and Dad have wanted to go back to Loch Lomond for years. It'd be five-star luxury all the way, no expense spared. Dad would get the break he needs and so would you.'

'Tempting, but no. I'm standing firm on what I said last year. Your father and I don't want any more of your money; we'd rather see more of you.'

'You're not still sticking to that stupid agreement, are you?'

'I certainly am. For every hundred pounds you want to give us, I want an hour of your time in return. I heard that's a pretty good deal for a major player like you.' She winked at him. Actually winked at him.

'Yes, Mum, but I'm supposed to get the money, not the other way round and, anyway, you've seen plenty of me recently.'

'The amount you've been away the last few years, I reckon you still owe me plenty.'

Not for the first time, Josh regretted that he'd got his stubborn streak from his mother. He was just going to have to find a loophole.

She gave him another one of those looks. 'Go and check on your father and see if he wants a cup of tea.' Josh started out of the kitchen but she called him back. 'And puts *this* back where it belongs!'

He grinned and took the cordless phone from her, then tiptoed back into the living room to place it in its cradle. Dad was snoring now. The paper was fluttering madly with every exhalation and Josh lifted it off him. Better to leave him. Dad needed his rest.

But there was only so much rest Josh could take. He was used to excitement. Action. Adventure. Yes, he wanted to be home and help Mum out while Dad recovered, but the biggest thrill he'd had in his six weeks here had been the rumour of a burglary at number forty-three.

He needed something to do before he went insane. Something he could do in London for a few days, just to stop himself going stark raving bonkers.

Funnily enough, it was as he was folding Dad's paper up to put it in the recycling bin that he noticed the advert, tucked away at the back. His adrenaline levels rose just reading it.

It was Tuesday already and she was still alive. Not only that, but she was starting to enjoy herself. Okay, she'd had a couple of meals she'd rather forget and had hidden behind her hands at a horror movie but, on the flip side, she'd unearthed a talent for salsa dancing. Who would have known her hips could swish and swirl like that? Even after one lesson she could feel the difference in the way she walked.

She smiled across the small round café table at Lisette and took another bite out of her wrap. Her friend had been on to something after all. Only she wasn't going to confess that to Lisette. It would only spark off another round of crazy ideas.

Still, she was looking forward to Sunday morning, when her life would be her own again. Only four more days. How hard could it be?

'Here's Simon now,' Lisette said, waving towards the doorway.

Fern turned round and smiled. Simon was a nice guy. She'd got to know him quite well, planning various fundraising activities for their local volunteer group.

'All set for tomorrow?' she asked as he pulled out a chair and crumpled into it.

He nodded and added a breathless, 'Yes' for good measure. 'Sorry I'm late. We had a last-minute person sign up to do the bungee jump and I had to sort out the paperwork.'

Lisette grinned. 'Is he hot?'

Simon looked blankly at her.

'Only asking!' She stood up and pulled her purse out of her handbag. 'I'm going to be decadent and have a triple caramel muffin. Anyone else want one?' She looked pointedly at Fern. 'Fern?'

See? This was easy, if not downright enjoyable. A guilt-free muffin. She couldn't say no, after all, could she?

'Yes.' She said the word slowly, giving it added weight, and Lisette's eyes lit up with a mischievous twinkle. 'I would love a muffin. Thank you very much.'

Simon coughed and shook his head. Lisette wiggled off to the counter.

'Fern?' His pale blond hair flopped over his forehead and he pushed it back. He was wearing his trademark *earnest* look.

'Yes, Simon?'

'I was wondering what time you'd be able to get there tomorrow to help with the registration forms and everything.'

'Okay. What time do you want me?'

Oh, dear! That had been such an innocent remark and still a blush crept up Simon's neck and stained his cheeks.

'I mean, how early do I need to be there?'

His hair flopped over his face again and this time he didn't bother to push it back. He shrugged and looked back at her through his fringe. 'Eight o'clock? If that's not too early?'

Actually, she'd been hoping that it'd be more like ten o'clock. This was the first day she'd taken off work in months and she'd really been looking forward to a lie-in.

'That's fine. It's all in a good cause, isn't it?'

Simon looked nervously towards the counter, where Lisette was flirting shamelessly with the barista. 'Actually, Fern, there's something I've been meaning to ask you…'

Uh-oh.

'Simon, I… Oh, look! Here comes Lisette!'

Her flatmate returned, grinning, with two caramel muffins and the barista's phone number on a scrap of paper. Just in time! She had a sneaking suspicion she knew what Simon had been about to ask her and she really didn't want to hear that question, not this week.

He was a nice enough guy: polite, sensitive, cared about other people. She guessed he'd been on the verge of asking her out for about two months now. Why, oh why, did he have to pick this week to pluck up his courage? They'd be together all morning tomorrow, organising the charity bungee jump, and she was sure this wouldn't be the last she'd hear of it. She knew she'd have to say yes to a date.

Would that really be so horrible? He was good company—a little intense at times, maybe, but he was fairly good-looking in a public schoolboy kind of way.

It was just that there was no *zap*. No chemistry. But, then again, she'd only felt that little lightning strike once in her life so far. She shook her head.

Zap didn't mean anything. It didn't mean long-term. It didn't even signal compatibility on more than a physical level. And it certainly didn't stop you getting your heart broken and withering away from an unrequited teenage crush. Zap, in other words, was dangerous.

No, Simon was a good choice, a safe bet. Maybe she *would* say yes when he asked, even if he stuttered and stalled until after midnight on Saturday. There'd be time to generate a zap. Sexual chemistry was supposed to be all between the ears, anyway. That was what Lisette had said after she'd finished reading her latest self-help book.

She unwrapped her muffin carefully and placed it on a plate. 'Simon says we need to be there at eight tomorrow, Lis.'

Simon shuffled in his seat. 'Actually, those who are actually doing the jump probably don't need to turn up until nine-thirty.'

Lisette, who had just bitten into her muffin—still in its case—swallowed and flicked the crumbs away from the corner of her mouth with a finger. 'Actually…' her voice was muffled as she chewed and swallowed her mouthful '…I have some bad news about that.' She scrunched up her face and looked at Fern through half an eyelid.

Oh, no. She had a really bad feeling about this.

'Don't look at me like that. "Bad Cop, Good Cop" want to do more scenes than originally planned and we're starting filming tomorrow instead of Thursday. It's not something I could have predicted and I can't afford to turn the job down.'

Simon looked panic-stricken. 'What about all your sponsor money?'

'Well, I had an idea about that…' She turned to look at Fern and Fern's skin broke out in goose-bumps. 'Fern, my old buddy, my old friend—'

Fern jumped out of her seat and pressed the fingers of one hand flat against Lisette's mouth.

No! No way!

Her voice was reedy and shrill, and much louder than she'd anticipated, when she finally got it to work. 'Lisette, don't you dare…!'

CHAPTER TWO

THE noise in the coffee shop instantly dropped to a dull murmur. A teaspoon clinked against a saucer. Fern froze and noticed that not a few pairs of eyes were looking in her direction. She sat down with a bump, her fingers still in contact with Lisette's lips in a vain attempt to hold back her question.

It did no good; Lisette just mumbled against them, her lips squashing into odd shapes. 'Will you take my place and do the jump for me?'

Fern glared at her flatmate. Slowly, she pulled her fingers away and folded her hands in her lap, never once blinking or breaking eye contact with Lisette. It was only when she heard a rustle to her left that she remembered Simon was still there.

'Would you, Fern?' he said meekly.

She turned sharply to look at him and he shrank back. Better downgrade that glare to a firm-and-in-control look. She took a few seconds to make the adjustment. Simon breathed out.

'Go on. Answer the man's question.' Was that a tremor she could hear in Lisette's voice? Fern flicked a look in her soon-to-be-ex-flatmate's direction. Lisette had the good sense to stop grinning.

She took a deep breath. Any other week and there was no way this would have even figured on her radar. A bungee jump! She couldn't do a bungee jump. What was Lisette thinking?

But the question had been asked and Simon was looking at her so hopefully. He was counting on her—the Leukaemia Research Trust was counting on her. And if she refused, they'd also lose out on the five hundred pounds Lisette had promised her if she fulfilled her stupid challenge.

She blew a breath out and let her body sag into the hard chair.

'Yes. I'll do it.'

Simon looked ready to hug her. After a few moments' awkward hesitation, he lurched forward and planted a wet kiss on her cheek. She looked at him. Not so much a *zap* as a *squelch*.

'Thank you so much! If you take Lisette's place we should still reach our target.'

She felt numb and could hardly listen to the rest of the conversation as Simon grabbed a cup of coffee and wittered on about how great it was going to be tomorrow. By the time he'd finished she only had five minutes of her break left. For the first time in her life she was going to be late back from lunch, because there were some things she needed to say to Lisette that just couldn't wait.

They both watched in silence as Simon mumbled his goodbyes and flapped through the coffee shop door, narrowly avoiding sending an elderly woman flying.

'There is no way I can do a bungee jump!'

'Yes, you can!'

'No. I can't.'

Lisette raised her eyebrows and pressed her mouth together in a rueful expression. 'Too late. You've already said you'll do it.'

Fern sighed and her brows crinkled together until a small crease appeared at the top of her nose. There had to be some way out of this. Some legitimate way that she could pull out without jeopardising all the money. Hang on a second…

She relaxed back into her chair and folded her arms. 'When we discussed terms and conditions, you said I could refuse to do anything dangerous.'

Lisette raised one eyebrow. 'Nice try, but the

jump has been approved health-and-safety-wise. You double checked all the paperwork yourself, remember? So why, if it's safe for all the other volunteers, would it not be safe for you?'

Drat! Caught out by her own efficiency.

'You don't have to do it, if you really don't want to.' Lisette scraped around her cappuccino cup with a teaspoon.

'I don't?' The sense of relief was like the sun coming out unexpectedly on a cloudy day.

The teaspoon made its way into Lisette's mouth upside down and she licked the foam off it. 'No one is forcing you to do anything. But you will forfeit my five hundred pounds and the four hundred pounds in sponsor money people have pledged me.'

Fern spluttered. 'Four hundred pounds! How did you manage that?'

'Remember that period drama I did last month when I was an eighteenth-century milkmaid?'

Fern nodded, not exactly sure where this was going.

'Okay, well, that corset made my boobs look really great. And there were lots of hunky male villagers with nothing to do but mill around for hours and stare at my cleavage…'

* * *

Josh ran up the escalator stairs two at a time and considered vaulting over the ticket barrier at the top. Under the watchful gaze of the London Underground official, he jammed his ticket through the machine and sprinted across the ticket hall and out on to the busy street.

He was late. Almost.

People were rushing past him, eyes down towards the pavement. He stopped and let them flow around him. Although London was technically home and, by definition, should be classed as boring, he couldn't help loving the bustle and excitement of the city.

He turned round on the spot, scanning the horizon. All those pavement-gazers took it all for granted. They weren't paying attention to the beautiful architecture or the clear blue sky criss-crossed with aeroplane trails, or even the two hundred foot crane towering by the bank of the Thames. He grinned to himself and set off towards it.

Good old Mum. She'd heard about this charity bungee jump from Helen Chambers and knew it would be just up his street. This was just for starters. Main course was the torn-out advert sitting in his back pocket.

He'd been working non-stop for the last six

months and desperately needed some fun. Why work hard unless he could play hard? He hadn't had time in his schedule to go snowboarding or white-water rafting recently. The South America trip would have been a good substitute, but he'd just have to have an adventure in London instead.

By the time he reached the foot of the crane, the first couple of volunteers had already jumped and another was dangling upside down while he was lowered to the ground. Josh scanned the crowd as he registered and started towards the little lift that would take him to the top of the crane.

He needed a partner for his next project and there must be at least one guy here who was up for an impromptu escapade. Someone physically fit with half a brain. Someone who'd be prepared to hare around the city for four days and possibly go home with five thousand pounds in his pocket.

Once he was at the top of the crane and waiting in line, he checked out his fellow jumpers more carefully. He made a little face to himself. Not really what he'd expected. A couple of senior citizens, a lanky guy with the look of a frozen rabbit and a few girls.

Another person jumped and the line shuffled forward. Seven more people to go and then he'd have his adrenaline high. There was nothing to beat it. He watched as the next volunteer had her ankles strapped into the harness.

She was standing stock still, staring out across the city. A lot of the others had clucked and fidgeted as the safety checks had been made, but not her. He tipped his head slightly on one side. Not bad legs either. And beautiful pale blonde hair that the wind was teasing bit by bit out of her ponytail. He allowed himself a small smile. Perhaps he'd try and get her number when they were both on terra firma again.

He liked his women brave and feisty. Sure, the relationships didn't last long, fizzling out quickly, but it was a heck of a ride while it lasted. He had a few more weeks to kill in London. Why not?

And then she turned to look back at the line of people behind her and he knew exactly why not.

He didn't need to know her number when he already knew her middle name. Not only that, but he knew that she hated Brussels sprouts, loved vanilla ice cream and had a tiny crescent-shaped scar on her temple. Knew it because he'd put it there accidentally when she'd been seven and he'd been messing around with an old tennis racquet.

Fern? Ryan's shy little sister was doing a bungee jump? He shook his head.

It was her turn to jump but she seemed frozen. A picture flashed in his brain—Fern, standing at the end of the diving board on a joint family holiday, her tiny arms clamped to her sides and her chin tipped up. He'd seen the look of fear in her eyes then and he didn't have to see all of her face to know it was there now. He knew what he had to do.

The other jumpers were starting to mutter and he pushed past them until he was standing directly behind her. She jerked her head round and a small croak came out of her mouth. Her eyes were glazed over and she hadn't even registered his presence.

He knew she'd kick herself if she didn't do this, just the same way that she had sulked for three days after he'd talked her down from the high diving board. Ryan had teased her mercilessly, forgetting—as Ryan conveniently often had—that it had been his goading that had forced her up there in the first place.

He stepped forward and placed his hands around her waist and whispered encouraging words in her ear. Exactly what words he wasn't sure, because all he could think about was how warm she felt beneath his fingers and how there definitely hadn't been that much curve there last time he'd grabbed her round the middle.

He'd done so many jumps like this he couldn't even count them, but he was pretty sure it was Fern's first time. So he carefully talked her through it, all the time trying to keep his voice steady and soothing, which was harder than anticipated, because he kept getting distracted by the smell of her hair.

He felt her muscles relax as he counted her down and then, before he could analyse the sudden urge to grab on to her and squeeze her close to him, she had fallen away from him and he was left hugging empty space.

He spread his arms wide—stretching to the tips of his fingers—lifted his face to the sun, rocked forward on to the balls of his feet and let gravity do the rest. A yell of pure joy erupted from deep inside his chest. He loved the first moments of a bungee jump, when the exquisite sense of freedom tangled with the natural human desire for self-preservation. Man, it was a rush!

He wondered if Fern had felt the same way. He hoped so. And, as the elastic tugged tight, giving him a split-second of stillness before he was propelled upwards again, he had an epiphany.

He didn't need a *man* to help him win the ten thousand pounds; he needed a woman. A woman who was clever and resilient and knew this city inside out. A woman he could trust.

He needed Fern.

The small stones on the dusty ground were starting to dig into her bottom, but she didn't care. She was going to be filthy when she stood up, but she didn't care about that either. All that mattered was that large sections of her body's surface area—namely, her rear end, legs and feet—were in contact with solid ground.

Her back was hunched forward and she was staring at her knees as she sat there motionless, dragging in deep breaths.

She'd never realised how much she loved the ground before now. She'd always taken it for granted—had stomped on it, had walked along it in spiky high heels, had generally ignored it. It had taken being spectacularly separated from it to make her realise how precious it really was.

After another minute she was ready to take her eyes off the dirt and focus on the horizon. The sight of the base of the great crane made her feel all fluttery again.

Had it really been Josh up there?

She deliberately kept her gaze level with the skyline, the sparkling office blocks and grand old buildings that dared to reach heavenwards. The bungee cord was free of any weight and swung aimlessly in the breeze. It must be over. She dragged herself to standing and brushed the grit off her bottom and the backs of her thighs with a few quick swipes of her hands.

That voice in her ear, those hands around her waist—had they been real? Now she was back with her feet planted on the earth it seemed like a half-remembered dream. She must have conjured the image up, been subconsciously taken back in time to a similar incident when he'd been there to help her. Funnily enough, in comparison, the memory of the diving board incident was fresh and clear: Bournemouth, over twenty years ago. That day, an unsuspecting eleven-year-old boy had won the eternal admiration of one small girl.

The murmur of voices behind her disturbed her thoughts. She put her hands on her hips and stared up at the crane.

He still had it. Her admiration. That and a bucketload more.

But she hadn't seen Josh in more than a year and he was more likely in Timbuktu or Bora Bora, working to put One Life Travel more firmly on the map. His mother was always boasting about her son's new millionaire status and the last time the Adamses and the Chamberses had had a get-together—without Josh, of course—Pauline had been full of Josh's new venture. Now, by helping charities organise and run expeditions, he could help hundreds of people every day, not only the people who took part in the expeditions, giving them an experience of a lifetime, but also the charities they raised money for.

Not that people really thought about raising money for an organisation. They thought about the people. People like Ryan. Wasn't that why she was here today? Why she'd agreed to this stupid challenge of Lisette's?

Thinking of stupid challenges and raising money, it was high time she made her way over to the registration table and got a signature to confirm she'd done the bungee jump. Then Lisette could go and collect all that cleavage-induced sponsor money. She smiled to herself. She was really looking forward to seeing Lisette's face when she handed her the form.

Above the general hum of conversation she heard a voice. 'Fern?'

It must be Simon. She wasn't surprised he'd come scurrying over as soon as he could. She pushed her hair out of her eyes and turned round, bracing herself for the *squelch*.

She was most magnificently disappointed as a fully-fledged *zap* hit her straight between the eyes.

Josh Adams! It had been real after all. Her mouth opened and closed.

As always, he knew just what to do and gathered her up into the most enormous bear-hug. Tears sprang to her eyes as the overwhelming ache of months spent missing him without properly realising it crashed over her. She buried her face in his shoulder, letting his T-shirt absorb the moisture.

A gentle cough somewhere to their right disturbed them.

Fern pulled out of Josh's arms, although their eyes were locked on each other and they were both grinning like maniacs. 'Simon, meet my old friend Josh,' she said, still staring and still doing the maniac thing.

Josh gave her a wink and tore his gaze away to look at Simon and offered him his hand. Fern turned to look at him too. Yep, there was the *squelch* she'd been expecting. It didn't even hit her right between the eyes. It just kind of wafted towards her half-heartedly and landed in a blob at her feet.

'Nice to meet you,' Josh said as he released Simon's hand. 'Are you Fern's…?'

Simon, who had been looking uncharacteristically tense round the jaw, brightened and opened his mouth to speak.

'Friend!' she blurted out, before he had a chance to mouth the first syllable. 'Simon is a really good friend of mine. He did most of the organisation for the bungee jump.'

Josh clapped him on the shoulder with the flat of his hand and almost sent Simon flying. 'Good man. In that case, let's get over there and sign these forms so the money can start rolling in. After that—' he looked at Fern and her tummy did a triple-flip '—I'm taking you out for coffee so we can catch up on the last few months.'

She raised an eyebrow. 'Try eighteen.'

He frowned. 'Has it really been that long?'

She nodded and gave him a rueful smile. How

could she forget that Christmas at the Adams's when he'd come home with the awful Amber? The darn woman had hardly been able to leave him alone. It had been embarrassing to watch her grope him over—and probably under—the table while they'd had Christmas lunch. Not that Josh had seemed to mind. Yes, that had been the year Fern had gone home early with a migraine.

He frowned again. 'In that case, I'd better buy you a really big coffee.'

'That's more like it. One with syrup in and whipped cream on top.'

Josh pulled a face, but she was undeterred. She was feeling rather fuzzy and low blood sugar was as good an explanation as any. Truth was she'd have drunk river water if it would give her a chance to spend a little more time with him before he dashed off to the next far-flung place. They'd been close once. Almost like brother and sister. Almost.

They had the kind of bond that didn't require constant telephone messages or texts, or even letters—and you could forget Christmas cards. She doubted Josh even had a list—but she'd seen too little of him in the last few years. It would be nice to have a chance to talk to someone who remembered Ryan.

Almost two decades had passed since her brother had died and the friends she'd known at the time were somebody else's friends now. And there was no point taking a trip down memory lane with her parents. They still found the whole subject far too distressing.

'Come on, then,' she said, tugging at his arm. 'There's a nice little coffee shop down by the river.'

Josh saluted her, then turned to smile at Simon. 'Don't you just love it when she gets all bossy like this?'

Simon opened his mouth to speak but no sound came out. In the end, he just nodded. 'Bye,' he croaked as they disappeared off the brown field site and joined the jostling city again.

Fern stood behind Josh in the queue at the coffee shop and tried desperately not to slide into a time warp where she was a shy thirteen-year-old harbouring a desperate crush on the boy next door. Unrequited, of course.

You're a grown woman now, she told herself. Enough.

But all her stern warnings couldn't banish the giddy feeling in her tummy when he turned round, winked and handed her a cardboard cup with a plastic lid. 'There you go. One large mocha with whipped cream.'

The giddiness upgraded itself into proper vertigo and she hadn't even got the sugar rush from the chocolate yet.

'Thanks.'

She knew what would happen now. She would drop her coffee, dribble it down her front or tip it all over him. Josh had always had this effect on her—at least since she'd had hormones in sufficient numbers for them to short-circuit her coordination. Since then, the warm, safe feeling she'd always got when he'd been around was counterbalanced with a jittery nervousness.

He'd always teased her for being clumsy, but the truth was she was only ever like it around him. And, after fifteen years of beating her hormones into submission, they had decided to stage one last revolt. Little traitors.

'Let's walk,' he said, nodding towards the door. She readily agreed. Morning coffee was blending into early lunch and the tables were packed tightly. Too many elbows and chair legs to avoid.

Once clear of the café, they crossed the road and ambled along the Thames Embankment. She loved the wide stone paths and solid walls, the outrageously ornate Victorian lampposts set at regular intervals. Bulbous-headed black fish gazed at her from the base of the lamps and wound their tails up the posts.

After walking for a few minutes in silence, they naturally gravitated to a quiet stretch of wall and stopped to lean on the smooth granite, their cups of coffee balanced in front of them. Josh nodded towards the crane poking above the skyline.

'That was quite a rush, wasn't it?'

Rush? Never had she felt such pure terror as when she'd been hurtling towards the ground, sure the bungee cord would snap or that her ankles would slide loose.

'Yes,' she mumbled, glad she had a good excuse to lie. Josh would never understand.

'I thought for a moment, when I heard you say no, that you were going to chicken out.'

Fern stopped watching the light play on the water as it lapped against the wall below her. 'I said *no*?'

Josh nodded. 'I think so.'

Fern bit her lip. Darn, darn, darn. All that for nothing! She'd shot herself in the foot before she'd even jumped. She felt like giving herself a hefty slap on the forehead, but that would have required an explanation she wasn't ready to give.

Instead she turned round and leaned her bottom against the cool stone and stared at the traffic racing along Victoria Embankment.

'Come on, Fern. Don't beat yourself up about it. Everyone is a little nervous on their first jump. It's only natural.'

She twisted just her head to look at him. 'Were you?'

He half-coughed, half-laughed. 'Well, no…but that doesn't matter, does it?'

Fern could feel the coffee churning inside her and looked down at her stomach. Yesterday, she'd been so sure this challenge of Lisette's was going to be a piece of cake and now she'd blown it. Stupid, stupid girl! All she'd had to do was say 'yes'. Such a tiny word. Not that difficult. Lisette was right; she was far too used to saying the opposite and a moment of subconscious muttering had cost the Leukaemia Research Trust nine hundred pounds.

'What you said up there doesn't matter,' he continued. 'It's cancelled out by the fact that… Hey, look at me…'

She looked sideways at him, her head still bowed forward. He raised his eyebrows, waiting. There was no point resisting Josh when he got all determined like this. She turned to face him and looked straight into his melting brown eyes.

'It's cancelled out by the fact that you did it anyway. You turned the *no* into a *yes* by your actions. And actions are what count.'

She blinked. That sounded a bit like wiggling out on a technicality. Could she just gloss over it? Tell Lisette she hadn't said no all week?

The smallest of smiles started on her lips, barely a curve. Focusing on the small print, Lisette hadn't exactly said she couldn't say the word no, had she? She just wasn't allowed to use it as an answer to a direct question. And she hadn't been asked a question on top of the crane. She'd been talking to herself.

It truly didn't count. A sigh of relief escaped her lips and she rested her elbows on the parapet once more. Josh's left forearm was only six inches away from her right one. Not close enough to suggest the intimacy of a boyfriend-girlfriend relationship, but close enough for her to feel the heat of him.

Josh moved the arm closest to her and gave her a gentle prod in the ribs with his elbow. 'What are you smiling to yourself about?'

'I really did it, didn't I?'

He grinned back at her. 'Yes, you really did. You were really brave.'

The smile waned and the crease reappeared between her brows. 'Don't be silly! I'm not brave, not like you. You must have done hundreds of those jumps.'

He sidled up closer so their arms were touching. The breath caught in her throat.

'You've got it the wrong way round. I'm not brave when I do a bungee jump. It doesn't take anything for me to do it. I love it. But you…'

The way he was looking at her, full of warmth and admiration, made her mouth dry.

'…I know you're not mad keen on heights. For you, it was brave.' One corner of Josh's mouth lifted in a smile. 'And that's why I have a proposition for you.'

CHAPTER THREE

FERN'S eyes widened. Was this it? The moment she had dreamed about as a teenager, lying face up on her bed, listening to power ballads and staring at the posters on the wall? Was this the moment when the scales would fall from Josh's eyes and he would finally see what had been under his nose all along? He was at least a decade behind schedule.

Her silly heart fluttered against her ribcage like a trapped bird. 'What…what kind of proposition?'

Josh leaned towards her, a glint in his eye, as if he were making her part of some thrilling conspiracy. He was close enough for her to see the olive-green flecks in his irises and catch a waft of his aftershave.

'I think we should spend a lot of time together over the next few days.'

'You do?' Her voice squeaked the same way it had every time she'd had to talk to him when she'd been a teenager. How embarrassing. All she'd been capable of doing back then was watching his lips move, hoping against hope that he'd stop mid-sentence, lean forward and…

As if he could read her mind, he came closer, near enough for the words he whispered to tickle her hair. 'How does five grand sound to you?'

Five thousand pounds? He was offering her money to go on a date with him? Didn't he know she'd do it for free? Heck, there'd been a time when she'd have given the contents of her savings account for such a privilege.

She shook her head. The lack of oxygen in all those high altitude places he'd trekked in must have interfered with his brain.

He suddenly stepped away and jumped up to sit on the edge of the wall overlooking the river. 'Don't say no before you've heard me out.'

A little laugh tickled at the back of her throat. God bless Lisette and her stupid bet!

'Come up here.' He held out one hand and patted the space on the wall beside him with the other. Now, climbing on walls was not something she normally did. They were usually there for a reason. In this case, a twenty foot drop with smelly river water at the bottom. But the look in his eyes told her it was easy—no big deal—and she placed her hand in his and wedged her trainer on the lip at the bottom of the wall. He tugged and for a moment she was airborne and then, somehow, she was sitting on the wall next to him, her feet dangling above the paving stones.

He reached into his pocket and pulled out a ragged scrap of newspaper. She squinted in the bright sunshine as he began to unfold it.

'You and me together for four days in London…' he muttered as he concentrated on flattening the paper out against his thighs.

Four days? This *moment* had definitely been worth the wait. Her chest seemed to expand, fill with sunshine.

Encouraged by her smile, Josh slapped the scrap of paper with the flat of his hand. 'I *knew* you were the right person to ask, the moment I saw you jump off that crane!'

Fern blinked. This conversation was not going anything like it had all those years ago in her daydreams. She'd always imagined that the realisation that she was The One For Him would hit him like a bolt from the blue, rendering him unable to anything but sweep her into his arms and declare his eternal love for her. In reality, it was an awful lot more confusing.

She turned to look at him, leaning forward and resting her weight on her hands as they gripped the edge of the wall. 'What *exactly* did you know when you saw me jump off that crane?' No harm in giving him a prod back in the right direction.

He looked puzzled. She raised her eyebrows and smiled softly in silent encouragement. Typical Josh. His quick brain would race ahead and, between one sentence and the next, his imagination would take so many leaps that he was on a totally different subject when he started to speak again, often so excited by his ideas that he'd forget that he hadn't said it all out loud and that those listening hadn't made the jump with him. Thinking outside the box was what he excelled at.

She summarised where they'd got to so far in the conversation, hoping it would jog his memory about what needed to come next. 'A proposition, remember? Five thousand pounds… you and me for four days in London…' Her pulse, which had calmed slightly in the last few minutes, started to panic again. 'What's this all about?'

He waved the piece of paper in front of her nose. 'The treasure hunt, of course.'

She snatched the piece of paper from him and held it still. Her heart had obviously banged against her ribcage once too often, because now it seemed to have slowed almost to nothing and she could hear the rush of the river in her ears.

'…and you want *me* to be your partner?'

He jumped off the wall and stepped in front of her. For a moment she thought he was going to take her hands, but then he fidgeted and stuffed them in his pockets. 'Yes.'

'Why?' The word came out like a strangled cough. She tried again. 'Why me?'

He stopped shifting his weight from one foot to the other and looked her straight in the eye. 'Because I think you'd be the perfect partner.'

Inside her head she was screaming with frustration. How many times as a teenager had she hoped to hear those words? That was the one thing he'd *never* been able to understand. But what he was asking her now wasn't what she'd yearned for back then. He had no idea he'd ignited a painful and distant memory.

Four days with Josh. Once upon a time, she'd have thought that was heaven; now she was starting to consider it more as purgatory. Being with Josh would be wonderful. And last week, if someone had told her he was coming home and she would get to spend some quality time with him, she'd have been thrilled. But last week she'd considered herself over that all-consuming teenage crush.

The adrenaline from the jump must have sent her system into overdrive, because now it was back with a vengeance and she was likely to say stupid things, do stupid things and, most dangerously, *feel* stupid things. For Josh.

It had already started. It was only an hour since they'd met again and she was getting all her signals crossed, imagining there'd be *moments* and bolts from the blue and—heaven help her poor confused heart rate—kisses.

Four days and she'd be in too deep to laugh it all off and pretend it didn't matter, as she had done the day after her sixteenth birthday party. Four days would be far too much and never enough. Not when he'd disappear off to Kathmandu or Papua New Guinea in a couple of weeks.

She shivered. Water slapped aggressively against the river wall behind her as the wake of a passing boat met solid resistance. Her fingers gripped tighter on the edge of the wall and she slowly slid herself down until her feet touched solid ground again. She pushed past Josh and folded her arms across her middle.

'Sorry, Josh. I can't.'

She was worrying the edge of her T-shirt with the tips of her fingers and Josh knew she wasn't as clear-cut about this answer as her tone and body language implied.

What was the problem? The treasure hunt was going to be a blast. And he knew Fern would have fun if she would just give it a chance. However, she didn't look as if she was thinking about how much fun it was going to be, with that faint scowl knitting her brows together. No, knowing Fern, she was worrying about something. Practicalities, probably.

Practical. That word described Fern perfectly. He remembered a time when she'd been six and had skipped up the garden and warned him and Ryan that the shed roof would never take their weight. He should have listened. His leg had been in plaster for six weeks and he still had a scar on his thigh.

So, he'd talk practicalities with her. Maybe then she'd give in to that little voice in her head he knew was just egging her on to say yes.

'The first prize is five thousand pounds cash and five thousand pounds in UK holiday vouchers.'

A slightly hysterical giggle erupted from deep inside her. 'Holiday vouchers? Why in heaven do *you* need holiday vouchers?' She paused. 'Come to think of it, you don't really need the cash either.'

'So why am I doing it?' See, this was why he needed her. They knew each other so well he could guess what she was going to say before the words left her mouth. 'Partly because it's going to be fun, but partly because Mum and Dad need a break and they won't let me pay for it. I've tried, really I have. But they might accept these vouchers. As you said, it's not like I have a use for them…'

Now he was frowning too.

'They're both so stressed. Dad is frustrated that he can't be the workaholic he knows how to be and Mum is terrified he's going to get bored and put himself in danger by doing too much too soon.'

The mini-scowl eased from her face a little. He decided to carry on while there was a thaw. 'I was planning to send them off to Scotland where they had their honeymoon. Mum's always said how good for the soul those mountains are.'

She smiled at him. 'That's a lovely idea.'

'And what about you, Fern? I'm sure you could

find something sensible to spend the money on. Pay off a bit of your mortgage or something. Didn't that Simon guy mention something about the Leukaemia Research Trust—' at this she perked up and he knew he was on the right track '—some appeal they're holding at the moment?'

'I expect he mentioned something like that,' she said quietly, the pull of conflicting emotions clouding her pale blue eyes.

He laid a hand on her arm, but stopped short of sliding it around her shoulders and pulling her to him as he had the urge to do. As he'd had the urge to do ever since his fingers had felt the soft curve of her waist before she'd fallen out of his hands. He suddenly felt very careless for letting her go that easily.

'Come on, Fern. The possibility of five thousand pounds and four days in my scintillating company. What's not to like?'

She shook her head, but couldn't help smiling. 'You always were a bit of a big-head.'

'And you used to say you didn't see enough of your honorary big brother.'

She shook her head. 'Seriously, I can't just drop everything. I have work to do.'

'What sort of work?'

'Well, my job involves site visits so I can assess risk factors. The insurance company then uses my report to decide the premium.'

'And how many visits have you got planned over the next few days?'

She unfolded and refolded her arms. 'Well, none actually—' she held up her hand to stop him interrupting '—but I'd really been looking forward to having a chance to clear my desk and catch up with the filing.'

He gave her an incredulous look. 'Sweetheart, filing can always wait for a few more days.'

She glared back at him. 'It's too short notice. I can't just not show up tomorrow.'

'Why? Have you used up all your annual leave?'

She opened her mouth and shut it again. Then she looked at the floor. 'Yes,' she said with the vague hint of a question in her voice. He knew that routine.

'Fern?'

She looked up.

'Are you fibbing?'

She blew out an exasperated puff of air and the slightly guilty look in her eyes made him want to chuckle. 'Yes.'

Their gazes locked and the urge to chuckle

leached away. 'You could ask your boss, couldn't you?'

She tutted and mumbled some kind of answer as she pulled a mobile phone out of her neat little brown leather rucksack. He tried not to smile too hard as she pressed a few buttons and walked away from him, holding it to her ear. He also tried not to stare too hard at her bottom as she took slow, steady steps away from him, deep in conversation with someone else.

When had Fern started walking like *that*? With all that sway and fluid grace? She wiped the smile off his face completely by turning round suddenly and catching him in the act. He tried to look nonchalant. Maybe she hadn't noticed.

He couldn't work out how the conversation was going. Fern wasn't looking pleased, but she was nodding more than she was shaking her head. Finally, she removed the phone from her ear, punched the button and took quick steps towards him.

'Well? Did he say yes?'

She sighed and nodded just the once. He swore that, as she tucked her phone away back in her bag, he heard her mutter something like, 'It must be infectious.' When she had zipped every last zip and popped every last popper she looked up.

'Come on, Fern. It'll be fun. What do you say?'

Half of her answer was muffled against his chest as he dragged her into a triumphant hug, ignoring his earlier instinct to keep a bit of distance. So he kept wanting to touch her. So what? What were impulses for, if not for following?

Fern was so used to the rumbles, screeches and hoots of the London traffic that she filtered it all out as she made her way from Embankment tube station up the Strand towards Trafalgar Square. Josh had said to meet him there at eleven-thirty and it was already twenty-five past. She picked up speed.

Gone were the glorious blue skies of yesterday. The weather forecast had said it was going to be overcast and for once it was right. Pearly-white clouds hung high in the air, robbing the light of its golden quality but doing nothing to reduce its brightness. She was squinting already, which meant she would almost certainly have a headache by the end of the day.

On the Internet last night she'd done some research on the event and had found out that it was called the Secret London Treasure Hunt, organised by London City Radio to promote not only their shows, but the famous tourist attractions. It had also said something about discovering interesting nooks and crannies that even many Londoners didn't know about. She smiled. This was really going to be her kind of thing.

She loved the history of London. Her office was in the square mile of the old city and she spent many of her lunch hours exploring the side streets, little parks and myriad churches. There was always something fascinating to find, some little adventure to go on.

There was more of a crowd in Trafalgar Square than she'd expected. She knew from the treasure hunt website that there were forty teams of two people each. As far as she could make out, that number would be reduced each day until only ten teams were racing for the finish line on Sunday. Of course, she could make life much easier for herself and lag behind, causing her team to arrive late enough to be eliminated at one of the checkpoints. She'd have done her duty to Lisette and Josh and she wouldn't be forced to spend the next four days with him.

But deep in her heart she knew she couldn't do

that. It would be too selfish. Josh's parents really deserved the holiday, and how could she deprive the Leukaemia Research Trust of the funds it so desperately needed?

She shifted the small backpack she was carrying so it was more comfortable on her shoulders as she crossed the road on to Trafalgar Square. The bag contained as much as she could carry for the next few days: a change of clothes, toiletries, her mini first aid kit. She thought she'd packed light but it was getting heavier by the second.

Where was Josh? She couldn't find him anywhere in this crowd.

In the end she decided to make her way to the small booth at the edge of the square where similarly dressed people were queuing up. Red Secret London T-shirts with the radio station logo on the back had been provided for all the registered teams. The air fairly fizzled with excitement.

She checked her watch just before she signed in. Eleven-forty. And Josh's extravagant squiggle of a signature was missing from the sign-up sheet. She took one last look over her shoulder, then neatly completed the form. There. She was committed now.

The man behind the desk offered her a sheet

of paper and she absent-mindedly took it from him as she turned and walked away, scanning the crowd one more time.

Where was he?

This was typical Josh. Perhaps something more exciting had come up last-minute and he hadn't been able to say no. One side of her mouth twisted up into a wry smile. How ironic.

A sense of disappointment bled into her body, causing sudden lethargy. Suddenly her backpack felt too heavy for her and she slid it off her shoulders and let it drop at her feet. She was starting to get really cross with Josh for making her feel like this once again. Overlooked. Not special enough.

Since she was the type of person who preferred to do things rather than sit around and mope, she decided the best thing she could do at this precise second was to be furiously angry with Josh. She yanked her backpack off the ground and started marching round the crowd, looking for him.

He'd better have a darn good explanation when he turned up.

Suddenly she stopped dead. Perhaps he did have a *really* good explanation. What if something had happened to his dad? She covered her mouth with her hand. He'd be devastated.

And it was as she was standing there, her heart pumping with the horror of all the possibilities, that she finally laid eyes on a familiar mop of sticky-up dark hair. She'd come full circle and was back by the registration booth. And there he was, propped up against it, a smile on his face and a familiar glint in his eye. That glint was legendary, and it meant that somewhere there was a—her eyes shifted to the right and she found what she was looking for—a woman.

How dared he be looking all calm and collected—and *glinting* at other women—when there was only ten minutes before the start of the race and it didn't even look like he'd tried to find her? The anger was back, bubbling up in her throat and making her feel as if her eyes had steamed up from the inside.

Looking forward to four days with Josh? Pah! She must be out of her tiny mind! The race hadn't even started yet and already her emotions had taken a roller coaster ride through frustration, despondency, fury, panic and back to rage again. This was what Josh did. He made life terrifying. And she'd signed up to four whole days of it!

Checking her anger, she walked deliberately up to Josh and the girl. Only as she came within six feet of him did he wrestle his attention away from the leggy brunette in a teeny-tiny Secret London T-shirt and shorts and look up. How many times must she have washed it to get it that small?

'Fern!' He looked at his watch, then gave her an indulgent look. 'You're cutting it a bit fine, aren't you?'

Fern was tempted to throw her head back and scream out her frustration. Of course, she did nothing of the sort. 'Actually, I've been here for ages, looking for you.' She raised her eyebrows.

He gave her a smirk that said, *Whoops! Sorry!* She shook her head.

'I got a little sidetracked talking to Kate here.'

She bet he had. She looked the other woman up and down. Long toned thighs, little shorts and a pair of rather obvious… assets, stretching against her tiny T-shirt. Kate had the whole Lara Croft thing going—without the thigh holsters and pistols. Of course Josh hadn't been able to tear himself away.

Somewhere behind them there was a scraping and screeching noise as somebody tapped the microphone rigged up to a PA system. 'Come on,' she said. Josh jumped up from his lounging position, suddenly energised, and followed her to the back of the crowd. Why was she not surprised that, when she glanced back, she caught Kate checking out his bottom?

A forty-something with glaringly white teeth, London City Radio's late night DJ, bounded on to a small platform set up near the base of Nelson's Column. A ripple of applause went through the crowd. Fern edged her way closer to the front, eager not to miss any of the details.

After a few minutes of good-natured banter with the crowd, he got down to business, calling the teams entered in the treasure hunt to stand in the space directly in front of the stage.

'Now, contestants, you all received a copy of the rules when you signed up for the treasure hunt and, just in case you've left them at home, we've supplied extra copies when you signed in this morning.'

Fern stared down at the half-crumpled piece of paper still gripped between her fingers. She'd obviously scrunched her fingers together a little too hard when she'd finally found Josh. She tried to smooth it out again between her palms. Rules. Good. One thing her life needed at the moment was a little bit of structure.

The DJ flashed another grin. 'But, just so

everyone is clear, we're going to go through the basics right now.'

Josh pretended to yawn and she dug him in the ribs with her elbow.

'The hunt starts at twelve o'clock today and will end at noon on Sunday. During that time, you will travel across the city, visiting both well-known tourist attractions and little-known historic sites. You will all receive a set of identical clues and a digital camera. Each time you solve a clue and reach the next destination, you will need to take a photograph to confirm you were in the right place. These photographs will then be shown to the team marshals at the end of each day. Sometimes the clue will be a riddle for you to solve in order to find the next clue…'

Fern smiled. She was good at riddles and lateral-thinking problems.

'…sometimes you will have to complete a task or perform a challenge before you will be given the next clue.'

Now Fern scowled and squeezed her eyelids together. Please, please, don't let there be another bungee jump!

'Fern?' The word was little more than a tickle of breath against her neck. 'Are you okay?' She nodded furiously and opened her eyes. Josh was standing right behind her, his fingertips resting on her waist as he listened to the DJ outline the rules. She missed a few sentences, too caught up in the little electrical charges travelling from the points of contact all the way up her spine.

She was reminded of that moment at the top of the crane—was it only yesterday?—when she had felt his touch and heard his reassuring whisper in such a similar way. Now, as it had done then, a peculiar sense of peace enveloped her.

The DJ was finishing up. 'By 10 pm each evening you will have to arrive at the specified checkpoint and the number of teams will be reduced by ten. Some teams will arrive late. Some teams may not have the correct sequence of photographs. These teams, along with those arriving last, up to a total of ten teams, will be…eliminated.'

He said this with such a sense of drama that the crowd stopped fidgeting and whispering and a hush descended. Even the ever-present pigeons seemed to fall quiet. 'Now, if the contestants can see the support team of special Secret London marshals—' he waved his arms to indicate the group of people dressed in a black version of the now familiar T-shirt '—we can provide you with the envelope containing the first clue and the essentials you will need for the race.'

Fern's heart started to beat faster. Josh grabbed her hand and dragged her forward. They found one of the T-shirted marshals, a girl who seemed to be all of fifteen. 'Mobile phones, credit cards and cash, please,' she said in an annoyingly chirpy manner.

Fern's hand flew to the mobile phone in her back pocket. 'My phone? My money?'

Josh was busy emptying his pockets. 'Weren't you listening? It's part of the rules. We get given Travelcards so we can have free travel on the underground and buses and we all start off with ten pounds for each team. That way, it's an even playing field. We can't call other people for help and those with lots of ready money can't use it to get ahead. Seems pretty fair to me.'

Fern clutched her phone. What if there was an emergency at the office? What if her parents needed her? Taking part in this treasure hunt was going to be a bit like being cut off from the rest of the world. Odd that, when they were in the middle of a city with a population of over seven million. She reluctantly plucked the cards and cash out of her purse and dropped them, together with her mobile, into a waiting plastic folder with her name written on it.

A few minutes later the teams were standing apart from the rest of the crowd, clutching their Oyster cards, a five pound note each and an envelope containing the first clue. She quickly looked around. The Lara Croft look-alike met her gaze. She was teamed up with an equally perfect male specimen. Apart from the obligatory red T-shirt, both of them were dressed head to foot in black. Some people were taking this competition just a *little* too seriously.

The DJ coughed into the microphone to draw attention to himself. All the contestants' heads swivelled towards him. Fern realised she was holding her breath.

'You may open your red Secret London envelopes…' a long pause followed; she was sure he must be counting to one hundred inside his head, because it seemed to go on for ever '…now!'

She tore at the envelope in her hand, but her fingers seemed to be thick and uncooperative. Other teams were already pulling the piece of paper out and reading the clue. She shot Josh a look of desperation and handed it to him. Josh, characteristically, didn't waste any time and ripped the whole thing open, actually tearing the clue in the process too. He had to hold the two bits together so they could read it.

> Make your way to Berwick Street market. There you will find ten stalls with the Secret London logo on them. Two teams may work on each stall. Your team must sell £30 worth of fruit and veg in order to receive your next clue. You may keep any money you make to help you in the treasure hunt. If all the spaces on the stalls are full when you arrive, you must wait for one of the other teams to complete the task and then take their place.

Fern looked up. A couple of teams were already running across Trafalgar Square towards the road, desperately trying to hail black cabs.

'Berwick Street. It's not that far from here, is it?' Josh said.

All she could do was watch the other teams sprinting away from them in random directions. She shook her head. Josh was looking this way and that.

'Nearest tube station?' He waved his hand in front of her eyes. 'Fern? Come on!'

She flinched. 'Um…' Her brain seemed to have sprung a leak. She knew the city like the back of her hand but, all of a sudden, she couldn't remember where the nearest tube was.

Josh grabbed her hand and started running off in the direction of Charing Cross station. Oh, she'd known that this was going to be a huge mistake. She hadn't even thought of that.

'I know some of the other teams are hailing cabs, but I thought we would do well to save our money for later,' Josh yelled at her between pants. The pounding of her feet, the sound of her breath rushing in her ears and the noisy traffic made it difficult to hear him even then.

She couldn't breathe. She couldn't even think. Panic welled up inside her. Josh seemed to sense that something was wrong because he turned his head, slowed a little and gave her hand a gentle squeeze.

Finally, she exhaled properly. She'd never been good at this kind of thing: pressure, deadlines, the feeling that time was ticking away and there was nothing you could do to slow its progress. It had been that way as long as she could remember.

Ever since she'd known that her older brother only had weeks to live. Terrified didn't even begin to define what she'd felt. And, even now, any sense of a high-stakes deadline had her sweating, living in a strange kind of emotional flashback.

She felt the pressure of Josh's fingers curled between her own and warmth seemed to seep into the cold spaces inside her. He'd been there for her then and he was here for her now. She began to run faster.

They rushed down the steps of the tube station, avoiding tourists staring at folded-up maps and ran towards the ticket hall. Thankfully, their Travelcards meant that they didn't have to queue up to buy tickets; they merely had to touch them to a pad on the barrier to open the gate.

Fern followed Josh to the top of the escalator. It was an unwritten rule that on the underground network, all those wishing to save their energy and enjoy the ride stayed to the right, allowing those in a hurry to double their speed by running up or down the escalator on the left-hand side. She didn't need to be telepathic to know that she and Josh weren't going to be standing still and admiring the scenery.

Luckily, a train arrived within seconds of them

bursting on to the platform and they jumped inside, grinning at each other and gulping in much-needed oxygen. Another team had been right behind them and had also managed to squeeze on to the tube train just before the door slid shut. She knew it was naughty, but she couldn't help chuckling as she saw three further teams skid to a halt and watch with dismay as the train hurtled into the dark tunnel.

Josh was holding on to the rail attached to the ceiling of the carriage, but he was restless, constantly twisting this way and that. She knew by the look of satisfaction on his face that he'd just had his first adrenaline surge of the day. The man was an addict.

The same chemical was throbbing through her veins. Only, in her case, it raced away, chaotic and uncontrolled. While Josh enjoyed the ride, she just couldn't feel the buzz, held too tight in the grip of the competition. With every heartbeat, she was willing the train on. *Faster, faster, faster.*

CHAPTER FOUR

FERN and Josh squeezed themselves out of the tube train doors before they had barely opened halfway and raced up the stairs and escalators of Oxford Circus tube station. Walking down Oxford Street, one of London's prime shopping areas, was hardly a gentle stroll at the best of times. In high tourist season, it was more like a rugby scrum.

'This way,' Fern yelled and set off running down a pedestrianised street beside the tube station. She glanced back over her shoulder and saw Josh hesitate for a second, then run after her.

It wasn't long before they were navigating the narrow streets of Soho. She stopped at a pedestrian crossing and pressed the button. Josh, who was already halfway across the street, stopped in his tracks.

'Fern! This is a treasure hunt, a race. You can't tell me you're going to stand there and wait for the little green man to flash?'

She blinked. She'd done it on automatic but it was hardly a bad idea.

'You can't take any chances with the traffic in this city,' she yelled back at him. 'Crossing the road, you're literally taking your—' she broke off as Josh leapt out of the way of a courier cyclist who had just bombed round the corner '—life in your hands,' she finished quietly, still staring after the cyclist as he mounted the pavement and disappeared down an alleyway.

'Come on! Live a little,' Josh shouted as he jumped on to the pavement on the other side of the road and started running again. Thank goodness the crossing signal beeped and flashed right at that very moment and she was saved from doing anything stupid. She sprinted across the road after him.

The noise of Berwick Street market reached them before they saw the stalls. Fruit and vegetable salesmen shared space with fabric merchants and dodgy-looking 'geezers' flogging second-rate electrical goods. She'd bet all the money in her pocket that one of those toasters would either burn the kitchen down or refuse to work at all.

The Secret London stalls were down near the

end of the road. Fern's mouth dropped open as they ran up to them and they both slowed to a jog. All the stalls were taken! How had the other teams got here so quickly?

She slapped her hand to her forehead. She was so stupid! How long had she lived in the city? How many lunch hours had she spent exploring it? A matching look of exasperation was on Josh's face.

'They came on foot,' she explained wearily. 'It's only a ten minute walk from Trafalgar Square to here—less if you run. We spent twice that jumping on the tube and running up and down escalators.'

Josh put one arm around her shoulder and gave her a squeeze. 'Never mind. We're not first, but we're not last either.'

She shook his arm off. 'Yes, but I should have realised! I *knew* it would be quicker on foot and the thought didn't even enter my head.'

She crossed her arms and turned away from him, scanning the stalls to see if any of the other contestants looked as if they were going to be finishing soon. Once again she'd proved that she was going to be as good as useless to Josh over the next few days. Why hadn't he listened to her? Why had he made her do this? He needed someone who was good under pressure, someone who loved the feeling of blood pumping in her ears and the adrenaline crashing through her system.

She spotted Kate, the Lara look-alike, fluttering her eyelashes and using her assets to help her sell cantaloupes. Much as she hated to admit it, *she* was the kind of partner Josh needed—a girl up for anything.

Let's face it, she told herself. You just don't cut the mustard. Usually, the biggest thrill of her week was trying a different flavoured syrup in her decaff latte. And, as much as she hated to admit it, that was just how she liked her life.

It was an agonising forty-five minutes before a space on one of the stalls was free. Fern tied on an apron with money pockets on the front. Looking at the other competitors, the idea seemed to be to try and copy the calls of the authentic fruit and vegetable sellers. Their sing-song shouts were almost like a foreign language. She stood in front of the stall and took a deep breath.

'Cherries! Seventy pence a pound.'

Pathetic. Her voice was little more than a croak. She sounded like a particularly timid librarian asking someone to keep it down.

'You're going to have to put a bit more welly into it if we're going to shift some of this produce,' Josh said, picking up a cucumber.

In her book, 'welly' was a big rubber boot you wore when it was raining. She sighed, then had another go at enticing someone to buy her bag of cherries. Nobody even glanced in her direction. She obviously didn't *do* 'welly'.

Josh gave her a wink, then let out a shout that drowned out half the other competitors as they struggled to make their allotted thirty pounds. 'Come on, then. Get your lovely cucumbers! Twenty pence each or three for fifty pence!' he mimicked the other market traders perfectly, but he hadn't finished yet—oh, no. He went right on into charm-the-pants-off-them tycoon mode.

'You, madam,' he said, pointing a cucumber at a portly-looking woman in a raincoat. She scowled at him. 'How about a lovely fresh cucumber? Good for the waistline—keep that lovely figure of yours in trim and, not only that, a couple of slices on your eyelids of an evening will keep those eyes sparkling.'

The woman stopped in her tracks and, just as Fern thought she was going to whack Josh with her shopping basket, she smiled. 'Go on, then,' she said. 'And you can chuck a couple of those tomatoes in as well—as long as they're nice and juicy, mind.'

'Madam,' Josh said as he loaded the produce into a brown paper bag and took her money, 'they're as juicy as I am.'

'I'll bet they are,' she replied and popped the bag into a shopping basket, then went off up the road smirking to herself.

And that was how the next hour went. Josh charmed the passers-by while Fern hovered in the background and took care of the money. Takings really went up when he started juggling the oranges and generally making a spectacle of himself. A small crowd even gathered.

Fern leafed through the notes in her money pouch and put the coins into piles to count them. They'd just about reached their target. 'Josh,' she whispered loudly.

But he didn't hear her. He was too busy betting a stocky-looking guy that he could juggle a banana, an avocado and a pineapple for a whole minute without dropping them. Fern shook her head furiously. What was he doing? If they lost the bet, they'd have to part with over half their takings and they'd definitely be in last place.

'Josh, no!'

It was too late. Money had changed hands and Josh was giving the pineapple a few practice throws. Fern crossed her arms and huffed. However, she couldn't keep up that stance for long as Josh got going. The pineapple was obviously five times heavier than the other items and his juggling routine, which had been so smooth and rhythmical, was now syncopated and clumsy-looking. The stocky guy stood back and looked smug.

The second hand on her watch was crawling. It crept round the Roman numerals on the watch face far too slowly. Twenty seconds. Ten seconds. Five…

Fern let out a gasp as the pineapple left Josh's hand at an odd angle. There was no way he was going to catch that—not with the avocado making a break for freedom in the opposite direction.

'No!' The shout had left her mouth before she even realised she'd planned on saying it. Josh instinctively turned to look at her, taking his eyes off the fruit, and everything went into slow motion. The stocky guy punched the air in triumph.

Fern lunged forward, aiming for a piece of airborne fruit—any piece, as long as she caught something. They couldn't pay for damaged stock as well as lose the bet.

By some miracle reflex, Josh turned again and dived to the left to catch the pineapple in his free hand. The avocado continued plummeting towards the dirty tarmac off to his right but, just as Fern was about to scream, he swung out his right foot, made contact with the avocado and deftly kicked it into his waiting hand to join the banana.

The crowd erupted in a cheer. Some people even threw change. The defeated customer grudgingly handed over a twenty pound note.

Whether she liked it or not, the blood was certainly pumping in Fern's ears now. She grabbed at the wad of notes and stacks of coins, sending a tower of fifty pence pieces flying.

Josh turned to her, flashing a *how about that?* smile. It seemed he'd been able to sell the pineapple, banana and avocado to an impressed onlooker. His grin faltered as he took in her expression.

'How much?' he asked, stepping closer, an overly casual look on his face. She glanced up from scraping the coins off the ground and snatched the twenty pound note from him.

'Over fifty pounds.'

Josh started to do a little victory dance, but

managed to contain himself. The vibes she was sending out must be hitting him thick and strong.

'Just take the darn photo, Josh,' she said, stuffing the cash into her pockets, then reaching into her backpack for the digital camera. She handed it to him and crossed her arms.

'Say *cheese*,' he said. He was being cheeky, but she saw a flicker of nervousness in his eyes. It was an old trick—one he'd used many times in the past. He'd always been able to jolly her out of her bad moods, but this time it just wasn't going to work. The result was a picture of some wonderfully vibrant fruit and vegetables, piled high on the market stall, and one grey and thundery-looking Fern.

Yes, she loved spending time with Josh—or at least the *idea* of spending time with him—but he played havoc with her nervous system on so many levels that being around him was never comfortable. She was always on edge, waiting for the next surprise.

They got one of the treasure hunt marshals to verify that they had collected enough money and were handed their next clue. Josh ripped the red envelope open and passed the card to Fern.

Fern looked at it and handed it back to him.

'Next stop, Hyde Park,' she said and picked up her backpack, carefully putting her arm into each strap without looking at him. 'Our best bet is to walk back up to Oxford Street and catch a bus down to Marble Arch.'

Josh started running but, rather than jogging, she decided to set off at a brisk walk. She'd collapse before the end of the day if she didn't pace herself. Josh could race headlong into everything if he wanted and end up burned out. Pretty soon he noticed she wasn't right behind him and waited for her, falling into step beside her.

'Fern? What's up?'

She turned to look at him without breaking momentum. 'I thought we were supposed to be a team.'

'We are!'

'Oh, really? Then how come you took an executive decision back there and did something without consulting me first?'

'What?' He stopped and placed a restraining hand on her arm. She shook it off and started walking again.

'That stupid bet.'

'It wasn't *that* stupid. We got an extra twenty quid out of it.'

'You took a risk, adopted a strategy without running it past me. That's not being a team player.'

He was silent for a few moments. 'Fern, I'm sorry. I didn't think. I suppose I'm so used to being in charge that it just didn't occur to me.'

She harumphed, but her anger had lost its fierce glare.

'I know it was a risk,' he continued, 'but it was a calculated risk.'

Now she laughed. 'Hah! Calculated, my foot! You just did it because it seemed like a good idea at the time.' Like he always did. Like he always would. At that realisation, something inside her let out a long, heartfelt sigh. It wasn't a life she could live.

'It paid off, didn't it?'

'Only just! If that avocado had been an inch or two further to the right, we would still be back there, flogging apples and in last place.'

The noise of the traffic increased as they turned into Oxford Street. There was a bus stop close by and they ran to it just in time to hop on a red double-decker bus. They squeezed their way down inside until they were standing near the exit doors, ready to jump off when they reached their destination.

Fern shifted so she no longer had somebody's elbow jutting into her spine. 'You don't have to take every opportunity just because it's there, you know.' She tried to keep her voice as low as possible, but loud enough for him to hear above the growl of the bus's engine. As usual, no one was talking inside the bus and she was aware of a few curious ears listening in to their conversation. 'Some of the risks you take aren't calculated; they are just plain stupid—like today, for example. You were lucky, that's all.'

Josh just stared at her, his face expressionless. They obviously weren't going to see eye to eye on this one. The bus paused at a stop and the doors whooshed open. As the passengers who needed to get off squeezed past them, they were pushed apart. She made an effort to soften her expression, add some warmth into her tone. When the doors sprang closed again, she edged closer to him.

'Okay, in the grand scheme of things, the bet wasn't the end of the world. Nobody died. Nobody's life was ruined. But one day, Josh Adams, your luck is going to run out. I just don't want to be there when it happens. I don't want to see you hurt.'

He said nothing, but the deadness in his eyes was swallowed up by a look of understanding. She felt an answering prickling behind her own eyes and he reached out to steady her as the bus lurched forward.

There were no other teams in sight as they reached Hyde Park. Fern didn't know if that was a good thing or a bad thing. The market challenge had separated the contestants into two packs of twenty couples. She hoped that this meant she and Josh were at the front of the second group.

Treasure hunt marshals were standing waiting with a specially marked Secret London soapbox on an area of concrete at the corner of the park—Speakers' Corner, so-called because of the oddballs and fringe groups that collected here on Sundays to exercise their civil right to air their views, however extraordinary.

And, although it was only Thursday, a crowd had gathered. She suspected that some of the people standing there were connected with the treasure hunt, the rest had heard the updates on the radio and had turned up to be nosy. The challenge was for each of them to get up and speak for three minutes on a subject of their choice. Three minutes! She almost wished there'd been a crane and a length of elastic instead.

Even worse, they had to make it convincing. If her speech wasn't coherent, she would just have to try again until she got it right. She shot a panicky look at Josh, but he was busy sliding his backpack off and dumping it on the floor. She'd been here before and the onlookers gathered with only one purpose—to heckle mercilessly. They were going to eat her alive!

Josh didn't even hesitate. He jumped on to the box, put his fingers in his mouth and produced an ear-splitting whistle. Half the crowd stopped to listen, the other half hurled insults and carried on talking.

'Many people wait for their turn here at Speakers' Corner so they can get up on their soapboxes—' he indicated the crate beneath his feet '—literally, and tell you what they believe in. I'm not going to do that. I'm going to ask you what *you* believe in.'

'Free beer!' someone yelled from the back. The crowd let out a collective noise, half-chuckle, half-cheer. He had their attention now. Josh looked straight at the joker.

'And what exactly are you doing to get free beer?'

The man shrugged and looked away.

'My point exactly,' Josh said, making eye contact with as many of the crowd as he could. Fern experienced a little shiver of electricity as he looked in her direction. 'We are all very good at moaning about what's wrong with the world, but supremely bad at doing anything about it, and I'm challenging you to buck the trend and get involved.'

He went on to tell the assembled bunch of loiterers, tourists and office workers on their lunch breaks how taking part in a charity expedition would not only give the organisation of their choice much-needed funds, but it would be a once-in-a-lifetime experience that would pop them out of their safe little bubbles and give them a greater appreciation of other cultures.

She'd been unfair to him when she'd told him off for taking stupid risks. Yes, the stunt with the fruit had been a little daft, but she shouldn't have issued such blanket disapproval for his way of doing things. Listening to him, it all fell into place.

Josh was, by nature, an energetic, go-getting, thrill-seeking kind of guy. But he wasn't the harum-scarum teenager she remembered any more. He'd managed to focus his natural energy—both his greatest strength and his greatest flaw—and do something positive and amazing with it. Suddenly she understood that without this side of his personality, he wouldn't be the wonderful individual he was. He wouldn't be Josh.

She looked round the crowd. He was doing brilliantly. Many of them were nodding as he spoke and he drew the remaining couple of hecklers into the discussion, neutralising their disruptive influence. And his competence just tied the knots in her stomach into double bows. She was going to have to get up and follow him.

The seconds were ticking away. What was she going to say? What did she believe in passionately? At this precise moment, she had no idea.

Next to Josh she just seemed boring. Okay, in her job she helped people, in a roundabout kind of way, making sure they were safe, but at the end of the day she closed the office door and went home without another thought. It was a job, not a passion. That thought was still whirling round her head as somebody nudged her. The soapbox was empty. It was her turn.

She placed one foot on it, testing its stability.

It wobbled. She looked up at Josh and he smiled and nodded her on. Using her arms for balance, she climbed on top of it. The crowd seemed to have quadrupled in size. And they were all looking at her, waiting for her to wow them. Suddenly she couldn't breathe.

Her heart set up a loud booming beat inside her chest. People began to shuffle, making disgruntled noises. And then everything became startlingly clear. There was one cause in this life that she was truly passionate about: eradicating the awful disease that had taken her brother's life before he'd had a chance to go out into the world and live it. And if Ryan had had the chance to be standing where she was now, he would have stood up straight and spoken from the heart. She lengthened her spine and took a deep breath.

'How many of you have lost a loved one to cancer?' she asked. A few people nodded; even more raised their hands. Those who were unaffected were in the minority. So she told them about Ryan, about his wasted life. About a cruel disease that seemed to pick its victims at random and suck the life out of them. A couple of times she had to stop and cough away the tears clogging her throat. No one heckled.

She told them about how terrified she'd been doing the bungee jump yesterday, but that she'd done it to raise money to fund new research. She urged them that, if they didn't have a cause they felt strongly about to get involved in, to pick this one. Finally, just as she was running out of words, one of the marshals nodded and she breathed a sigh of relief and stepped down off the box.

Josh instantly wrapped his arms around her and squeezed her tight. 'You were great. That took a lot of guts.'

Fern didn't say anything. She was a fraud.

It had sounded great, talking about bungee jumps and being brave for what she believed in, but the truth was, without Lisette's challenge, she wouldn't have done it. She was such a hypocrite.

As Josh collected the next clue, she rubbed her face with her hands. She'd been prepared for this treasure hunt to be physically demanding. What she hadn't counted on was how emotionally draining it would be. The race was like a mirror, reflecting her life back at her. She'd taken a long, hard look and she didn't like what she saw.

Josh flicked through the clues that had led them back to the corner of Trafalgar Square as Fern snapped a picture of Canada House with the digital camera. From Speakers' Corner, they'd made the short hop to Marble Arch and climbed right up inside the orphaned gateway, now marooned on a traffic island at the point where Oxford Street met Hyde Park.

As far as he had known, it was made of solid stone but, sure enough, they'd found an entrance and climbed right up to a room at the top to find their next clue. Odd, how you could think you knew something well and yet you had no idea of the obvious truth that was right under your nose.

'Done,' Fern said and carefully stowed the camera away in her backpack.

Something was up with her. She'd been very quiet since the task at Speakers' Corner. Perhaps she'd noticed that he'd walked away out of earshot when she'd got going on her speech.

He hadn't meant to desert her, but he just hadn't been able to stay. As soon as he'd heard her talking about Ryan, her voice going all husky, he'd had the irresistible urge to move his legs. Maybe she was braver than he was. Maybe she could let herself talk about Ryan. Heck, he couldn't even think about his friend without wanting to jump up and do something—anything. Life was too short to sit around moping. He'd promised himself years ago that he wouldn't waste a second.

Fern read the clue she'd got from a Secret London clue box standing in the lobby of Canada House:

> Take in the sweet sight of one of London's best-known art galleries and find the Constable river scene showing Farmer Lott's cottage with people and livestock in the foreground. Check the room number, then go to the room that is four numbers higher to find a painting of four flowers, two the same.

They both looked up and stared at the National Gallery, which stood on the north side of Trafalgar Square.

'What are we waiting for?' he asked and they ran across the square, darting through the groups of tourists gathered round Nelson's Column, scaring a flock of pigeons in the process.

Once inside, Fern whacked him on the arm. 'Look!'

Straight ahead of them, looking this way and

that and then sprinting off into a side room was Kate, the girl he'd chatted to earlier, and her brother Aidan. Josh ran up a small flight of stone steps, stopping on a brightly coloured mosaic, and watched them make their way through one of the many rooms of paintings, stopping to scan each one before running on again.

They'd been one of the first teams to leave the market this morning. He grinned. This must mean his team was making headway. There were staircases in front of him and to the right and left. He picked the one on the left and started running up it, partly because it happened to be the one he'd been looking at and partly because it was the way Kate and Aidan had gone.

By the time he was two stairs from the top he realised something was missing—the sound of another pair of feet following him. Where was Fern? All day he'd been able to hear her steady footsteps behind him like a heartbeat.

He pivoted round and spotted her talking to a guide in the entrance hall. She waved a gallery plan in the air and pointed to her right. He jogged down the steps, met her at the bottom and then they ran up an identical flight of steps heading in the opposite direction.

'Constable's paintings are this way,' she said in gasps. 'You were about to look at paintings around two hundred years too early.'

'Really? That's the way the other team went.'

'All the better for us if they're headed in the wrong direction. *The Hay Wain*—a river scene and Constable's most famous painting—is hanging in room thirty-four!'

He felt like grabbing her and kissing her, but thought he'd better not.

Of course! His Aunt Beryl had a set of dog-eared place mats printed with the very same picture. He could see it so clearly in his mind's eye. The river, the cottage… It was just what they were looking for.

They ran through a few rooms of paintings and he glanced around, looking for river scenes or flowers. Thankfully, Fern seemed to know where they were going. Each room had a large central square arch leading into the next section of the gallery. Sometimes there were side openings as well, but she was heading straight through from one room to the next. That was until their progress was blocked by a locked door and a rather stony-looking guide.

'Sorry,' she said, peering over the top of her

thick-rimmed spectacles. 'This part of the gallery is currently closed.'

He looked at Fern and she at him, mouths open, and then they looked back at the guide.

'Not room thirty-four?' he said.

She shook her head. 'No. Rooms forty-one and forty-two. Thirty-four is…'

They didn't wait to hear the rest. Fern had the map in front of her nose again and a split second later she took off back the way they'd come. He raced after her. They took a right. And then another one. And pretty soon room thirty-four was straight ahead of them.

There, filling a large space on the deep red wall, was *The Hay Wain*. Fern ran over to the display caption and then grinned back at him. '"Painting of a farmhouse belonging to Willy Lott, one of Constable's father's tenants…" It says it right here!'

He took one last look at the painting. It was all there: the river scene, the livestock—well, horses—and the people. Josh was so excited he considered *whooping*, but decided it probably wouldn't be popular with the museum officials.

'So the other painting must be in room… thirty-eight.'

Fern nodded in agreement and glanced at the map again. 'That way!'

They dashed back through the entrance they'd just come through and kept on running until they found the right spot. Now he didn't want to *whoop* any more; again, he wanted to grab Fern and kiss her in jubilation. His veins were fairly buzzing with adrenaline. Who would have known that rushing round art galleries could give you the same high as snowboarding?

Then the buzz fizzled into nothing, just as instantly and completely as if someone had pulled the plug on him. Room thirty-eight was small and square and covered entirely in paintings of—

'Venice!' Fern exclaimed. 'Every one of them is a painting of Venice! And not a flower in sight. Are you sure this is the right room? Number thirty-eight?'

He looked up at the wall. There it was, in big, bold numerals.

'I don't get it.'

At that moment, a pair of identical twins in familiar red T-shirts skidded into the room, looking frantically this way and that. Josh grabbed Fern by the arm and tugged her into the next room, which overlooked the main stairway, separated by a row of glazed doors.

'Josh! What are you up to?'

He opened his mouth to speak, drawing in air, but stopped short. It was his turn to whack Fern on the arm to get her attention. Two more teams dashed through the entrance hall from one side to the other. Only seconds later, another team barged past him and ran down the stairs towards a guide and proceeded to have a rather heated conversation with him.

'The whole place is filled with treasure hunt competitors running around like headless chickens. At least it's not just us who can't find the right painting.' He shook his head. 'There must be something wrong with the clue. Maybe it's supposed to be "four numbers lower" or "five numbers higher", or six…or seven…'

She fidgeted under the weight of her backpack. 'In other words, it could be anywhere.'

She was right. And there was only one possible approach.

'We're just going to have to go about this systematically,' he said. 'Start in the section of the gallery we've just been looking in and eliminate paintings room by room.'

She nodded. 'Okay. Let's start back where we first came off the main staircase.'

They searched a handful of rooms. Plenty of river scenes. Plenty of flowers—sunflowers, water lilies—but nothing that matched the clue. They were getting nowhere. Pretty soon they were standing looking at *The Hay Wain* once again.

'Josh? Have you got the clue there?'

He pulled it out of his pocket and handed it to her, all the while staring at the canvas in front of him. The adrenaline rush had definitely subsided. Now he felt like a hamster on a wheel—endlessly running, but never getting anywhere. It was so frustrating. He hated staying in the same place, marking time.

'I've got it!' she said breathlessly. 'Look at this…it says "one of London's best-known galleries". It doesn't say this one. We just assumed it meant here because we were standing right outside it.'

The sheer logic of what she was saying hit him like a hard slap on the forehead. 'If not this gallery, which one?' He racked his head. The National Portrait Gallery was next door, but it hardly seemed the place for river scenes and flowers.

Fern began to laugh. 'Oh, they are *so* sneaky! The National Gallery is a complete red herring!'

It was?

She prodded the card with her finger. 'It says "take in the *sweet* sight". I didn't think anything about it at the time, but it's part of the clue! Sweet! What is sweet?' she asked, her eyes full of humour and quick intelligence.

You are, he wanted to say. Especially when she was all fired up and glowing as she was this very second. Thinking she was sweet was okay, wasn't it? It was certainly a big-brotherly kind of reaction. Much better than *desirable* or *incredibly hot in those jeans* or…he watched her lips purse into the tiniest of pouts… *kissable*.

'Josh! You're not listening!'

No. He was too busy looking instead. And he didn't seem to be able to stop looking at her mouth. She whacked him on the arm again. That did the trick nicely. He was going to be black and blue by the end of the treasure hunt, especially if thumping him was the only reliable method of distracting him from…

Pain exploded in his upper arm once again.

'Wake up, will you?'

He rubbed his arm as she continued talking, almost too fast for him to catch the words.

'Sugar! Sugar is sweet. And which major London gallery was founded by a sugar tycoon?' She raised an eyebrow, willing him to catch on.

'The Tate!' he yelled, then remembered how many other teams might be within earshot. 'The Tate,' he said again, whispering this time.

Now they were both chuckling.

'We might be in completely the wrong gallery…' he said as he guided her through the glazed doors and down the main staircase. They stayed well back as another few teams raced this way and that and decided to slip out of the gallery through the gift shop, rather than using the main entrance. '…but at least almost all the other teams are just as lost as we were.'

They looked around, then quietly left the gallery via the gift shop entrance, making sure they weren't followed. The large paving slabs outside were slick with rain when they emerged, the shower having come and gone while they'd been racing around the gallery.

'You, my sweet Fern, have just given us what we need to get into the lead.'

And then, before his impulse control facilities woke up enough to stop him, he planted a big juicy kiss on her lips.

CHAPTER FIVE

THEY made the tube ride in complete silence. Josh was wearing that intense expression he always wore when he was focused completely on something.

He'd done it again. Kissed her.

To say she hadn't wanted him to would be a lie. But since this was a good week for muddying the clear waters of truth, she wasn't going to admit to that. Instead she was going to focus on two positives: number one, this time she hadn't been actively wishing for it, practically willing it to happen and, number two: this time she hadn't kissed him back. She'd just stood there, as responsive as the brass Nelson spying down on them from the top of his column.

It had been more than a decade since the last…incident… and she'd obviously learned something from the previous encounter. Maybe, if he tried it in another ten years, she'd have the good sense to slap him round the face and tell him to stop mucking her about.

She let out a huge sigh, so loud that Josh turned his head to look at her.

'Okay?'

She nodded—briskly, brightly. 'Yes. Just tired,' she said, trying not to cringe. Now she'd passed from sidestepping the truth to out and out 'porky pies'. Josh seemed happy with her answer, anyway, and returned to staring out of the window into the blackness of the tube tunnel.

Soft, fluffy feelings were floating around inside her and she let them harden into a solid ball of resolve. No, there would be no silliness this time. No repeat performance of the embarrassment after Josh had kissed her on her sixteenth birthday. At least today's kiss had only been a peck in a moment of exhilaration, lasting no more than a second. Ten years ago, it had been a *real* kiss. One with honest-to-goodness fluttering and tingling that had left her sighing for hours afterwards.

The urge to sigh must be similar to the urge to yawn because, as soon as she thought about it, she did it again. She covered her mouth with her hand and tried to camouflage it as tiredness for Josh's benefit.

At sixteen she couldn't have known any better. At sixteen she hadn't realised that fairy tales were just fiction, that there was no way that Josh, three and a half years her senior—gorgeous, dynamic and about to go off to university and unleash himself on the female population of the campus—would ever be seriously interested in a mouse like her.

The aftermath had been too humiliating. The 'it's just bad timing' speech, followed swiftly by the whole 'age difference' thing… She shuddered at the memory. Embarrassing at the time, but ultimately the right decision. It hadn't been just her age and his physical proximity—or lack of it—that would have made it a bad match. Just look at them now.

He was the high-flying businessman, jetting over the world, never stopping long enough to put down roots and she was…well, wedged firmly in her nice little rut and enjoying it. Most of the time.

Back then he'd seen the bigger picture and had spared them both pain. The sooner her obstinate hormones cottoned on to that fact the better. Mercifully, at that moment, the tube doors sprang open and prevented her from reliving any more of those long-buried memories.

As they ran out of the tube station and headed towards Tate Britain, she tried to get her brain back into the present. The clues. The treasure hunt. They paused on the kerb of Vauxhall Bridge Road—even Josh wouldn't attempt to nip across four screaming lanes of traffic—and Fern plucked the clue card out of her pocket and took a look while she waited for the lights to change.

There were plenty of Constables in the gallery, but the flowers…

Suddenly, she became aware of engines growling impatiently, aware of Josh moving across the road and her own instinctive move to follow him.

…four flowers, two the same…

Someone leant on a horn and revved their engine loudly.

'Fern!' There was a hint of panic in Josh's voice. She looked up to find that she was standing still in the middle of the road, the red man on the pedestrian crossing signal glaring down at her. She turned her head just in time to see an equally enraged taxi driver mouth something she was very glad she couldn't hear through his windscreen. Finally her feet moved and she sprinted across the road to join Josh.

'I know this is going to sound a little odd coming from me, but I really think you should pay more attention when you're crossing the road.'

She waved the clue in front of his face 'I know!'

'Could have fooled me!' he said, stepping back slightly.

'No…' She batted his reprimand away with a flick of the little card. 'I mean, I *know*. I know which painting we're trying to find—the flowers!'

Josh grinned at her, but she didn't stop to smile back; she just started running. There was no way she was going to give him a chance to plant another kiss on her. Her hormones would just be getting mixed messages.

There wasn't much he could do but give chase. Unfortunately, or maybe fortunately—it depended which way you looked at it—he had a prime view of Fern's bottom as he jogged behind her. Not at all conducive to big-brotherly-type thoughts. Not one bit.

He picked up speed until he was running abreast with her. There. That was much better. Now he could only see the faint flush in her cheeks, the slight sheen to her face and chest… Oh, hell.

A lamppost appeared out of nowhere and he

had to duck sideways to dodge it. He should be keeping his mind—and his eyes—fixed firmly forwards on the paving slabs in front of him.

Fern seemed to know where she was going when they got to the gallery. She ran up to the desk, pulled a map of the gallery from a pile, then headed up a flight of wide white marble stairs. If the view of her rear end had been distracting before, now, from this angle, it was positively hypnotic.

He growled inwardly. It was all his own stupid fault, this sudden obsession with forbidden fruit. If only he'd resisted the urge to kiss her earlier on. He hadn't expected the jolt of electricity when their lips had met. It was still thrumming through his system, making him full to overflowing with restless energy. He should have curbed the desire, should have remembered just what effect the taste of her lips could have on him, because he'd experienced it once before and it had been a bad, bad idea then. Judging by Fern's response to his impetuous peck on the lips, it was an even worse one now.

She'd just stood there and stared at him, not like before, when she'd melted against him, had driven him wild by tentatively running her hands over his back, then bringing them up to thread through his hair…

Yeah, this is just the kind of focus you need to win this race, he told himself. Less than a second of up-close-and-personal with Fern—his honorary kid sister, for Pete's sake—and everything else had gone out of the window.

He skidded to a halt, then snapped his head first left then right. Finally, he'd managed to distract himself from looking at Fern's derrière but, in the process, he'd lost her completely. He was standing alone in a room full of sixteenth century paintings with only an unimpressed security guard for company.

At that moment, Fern's head appeared from beyond a large green and black marble archway at the end of the room. 'Josh! Come *on*!' she mouthed and waggled a hand to speed him up. He took off again and caught up with her in room ten, a small square space filled with Constables in different shapes and sizes. Instantly, they split up, scanning the display captions of each painting until they met up again on the opposite side of the room.

'Nothing here. Didn't you say you knew which flower painting the clue was hinting at? Do we actually need to find the Constable first?'

'Yes. We wasted time jumping to conclusions the last time. This time we're going to make sure.' She pointed in the direction of room eleven. 'There are more in here, by the looks of it.'

They repeated the process in the next room and, halfway up one side, he found a tiny canvas and knew he'd struck gold.

'I've got it!'

She dashed across the room and read the caption aloud: '"*The Valley Farm.* This work shows a view of Willy Lott's house at Flatford from the River Stour…"'

As she finished reading the caption, he pulled the map out of her hand and unfolded it. *The room that is four numbers higher…*

He pointed back towards the room they had just come from. 'Room fifteen is this way.'

'I know,' she said, giving him the first proper smile since his stupidity in Trafalgar Square. 'I was right. I know which painting the clue is pointing to.'

It was only a matter of thirty seconds before they were standing in a room full of Pre-Raphaelite canvases, staring at a dusky garden scene containing two little girls lighting Chinese lanterns. He scratched his head. 'Are you sure? There are way more than four flowers in this picture. There must be hundreds.'

'Yes, I'm sure. Look at the title: Carnation, Lily, Lily, Rose. Four flowers, two the same—get it? It's one of my favourites, but I didn't think of it at the time because we were assuming the clue was hinting at the National Gallery.' She raised her eyebrows and gave him a knowing look. 'Just goes to show where jumping in with both feet without thinking things through will get you.'

He felt his face heat a little. Was she trying to tell him something?

He held out his hand, a silent gesture requesting the camera. He knew she'd know exactly what he meant. But the camera stayed firmly lodged in her backpack.

'Didn't you read the small print on the clue?'

'Small print?'

'Always read the small print,' she said, producing the card from her pocket. 'We're not allowed to take pictures in the gallery, so we need to go and get a postcard of this painting in the gift shop and take a picture of one of us holding that. The cashier will give us the next clue when we buy the right card.'

'Oh.'

So much for *focus*. At present, he was about as focused as one of his mum's famous sponge puddings. He picked up speed and hurtled off in the direction of the gift shop. Moments later, Fern was standing beside him, fishing coins out of her pocket and the cashier was handing him a little paper bag with both the postcard and a red envelope inside it.

He smiled at the cashier. 'Are we the first ones to buy one of these cards today?'

The girl shook her head. 'I've sold three so far. One to a group of Japanese tourists first thing this morning, another to a girl and a guy like you—' she nodded to indicate their Secret London T-shirts '—and this one to you two.' She gave them an apologetic shrug.

Fern put the stray coins back in her pocket. 'Could you tell us how long ago you sold the second one?'

The girl's chin crinkled as she considered her answer briefly. 'Five minutes, maybe?'

He and Fern looked at each other and wordlessly sprinted in the direction of the front entrance. Once outside, he took a slightly wonky photo of Fern holding the postcard and then they ripped the envelope open.

'Back to the underground,' he muttered, and they set off running.

Just as they turned the corner on to Vauxhall Bridge Road, he spotted a pair of red T-shirts far on the other side of the road, running in the direction of Pimlico tube station. Kate and Aidan. Fern gave a disgruntled, *'humph,'* and he knew she recognised them too.

A flash of red—there!—disappearing up the stairs from the tube station on to the main concourse of Waterloo railway station. Fern craned her neck to get a better look as she rode the escalator.

'I think we're gaining on them,' she said to Josh, who was standing right behind her, but kept her eyes on the spot where she'd sworn she'd just seen a red Secret London T-shirt.

Kate and Aidan. It had to be.

They'd been playing a game of cat-and-mouse with the other team all afternoon. Sometimes she and Josh got *so* close, but the other pair always managed to maintain their lead.

She wasn't sure what was worse: not being able to catch a glimpse of them and, therefore, not knowing how far behind they were, or being close enough to see Kate jutting her chest out and sending Josh sly smiles when she thought Fern wasn't looking.

The steps of the escalator flattened out and Fern ran to the barrier and slapped the touchpad with her Travelcard.

The board on the main station concourse told them the train they needed left in just two minutes. She could now see Aidan and Kate clearly, as they raced away towards the platform. Josh started to give chase.

'Wait!' she called him back and pointed to an automatic ticket machine. 'Our Oyster cards don't cover the rail network. We need tickets.'

Josh looked wistfully after Kate's shapely, tanned legs as they sprinted out of sight. 'But we won't make it.'

'Yes, we will,' she said, already jamming coins into the machine. After the longest three seconds in history, it spat out a pair of identical yellow and orange tickets. She scooped them up and soon they were on the other team's tail. By the time they reached the barrier, her lungs felt as if each new breath was slicing into them and her legs were screaming for mercy.

Kate and Aidan were shouting at a station guard who was pink in the face and pointing back in the direction of the main concourse. She and Josh didn't even slow down as they slipped through the barrier waving their tickets. A whistle sounded. The train was leaving. Now.

A sudden burst of energy exploded through her and her legs pumped faster. They jumped through the hissing double doors just as they started to close, then pressed their faces against the window to look back up the platform. Kate and Aidan had stopped arguing with the guard and were just staring after them, faces like thunder.

Josh shook his head. 'You've done it again!'

She couldn't help grinning back at him.

'It was fate that we met up at the bungee jump this week. Fate that brought us together for this race and, boy, am I glad!' He collapsed on to a bank of empty seats and rested one foot on a seat opposite.

The grin on her face turned brittle and dissolved.

Fate, my foot!

It hadn't been fate that had brought her here; it had been Lisette's stupid dare. Josh thought she was brave and feisty and all the things a twenty-first century woman was supposed to be, but, in reality, she was nothing but a fake.

Oh, she wanted him to think that she was fabulous, but the reality didn't live up to the hype. Who was she really? Rut-girl, that was who. And, although the whole 'rut' thing had started as a joke, she was starting to see the wisdom of the old saying: *many a true word spoken in jest.*

Besides, she didn't believe in fate. If there were such a thing as fate, it was a cruel, malevolent force, because that would mean that, somehow, for some reason, Ryan had been *meant* to die. And she couldn't believe that. Wouldn't.

No, fate had had nothing to do with that. And it had nothing to do with the treasure hunt either. They'd used their heads and got this far under their own steam. Funnily enough, after all her grim thinking, this single thought warmed her. She'd done something exciting, acted quickly, used resources she'd buried so long ago she'd forgotten she possessed them.

And it felt good. No, it felt great.

This morning, she'd been happy to trail around after Josh as she'd always done, as if he was still the worldly-wise nineteen-year-old and she was the innocent, day-dreaming sixteen-year-old. She realised now that this particular dynamic had flavoured their relationship for the past decade—her idolising him and him only half-noticing she was alive.

But, in the course of a day, things had changed.

Their relationship had matured at rocket speed and he was no longer the glowing hero. No longer perfect. He was *Josh*. And that made him all the more appealing.

A warm, fuzzy sensation skittered over her skin. She felt liberated. Giddy, even. The glass wall that had always been between them had vanished and, if she wanted to, she could reach out and touch him now. The knowledge gave her a heady sense of power. A rush.

Without analysing what she was doing, or why she was doing it—and that *had* to be a first—she flopped down next to him, half on top of him, so her back pressed against his side and her shoulder fitted neatly under his arm. She sank back into him and propped a leg up on the seat next to her so her foot stuck out into the gangway.

It was the most natural thing in the world for him to move the arm he'd rested along the back of the seats and drape it across her body, co-cooning her to him. Somewhere inside her head, only just audible, the word she'd feared all week repeated itself over and over.

Yes. Yes. Yes.

* * *

They arrived, breathless, at the checkpoint and smiled hopefully at the treasure hunt marshal. He grinned back at them. 'Eight minutes past eight. Congratulations, you're the first to arrive.'

Fern waited for Josh to pull her into a bear-hug, but he just jumped up and down on the spot and held his hand out for a high-five. She obliged by giving his hand a half-hearted slap.

Now that they were no longer actually racing, they took in their surroundings. The checkpoint was in a gravel car park in a leafy suburb of south-east London. A large wooden sign proclaimed they were standing outside Chislehurst Caves.

'I didn't know there were caves in London,' Josh said as the marshal led them in to the entrance. Instantly, the temperature dropped and the air was thick with the smell of damp. Instinctively, Fern reached for Josh's hand.

As the guide led them deeper into the cave network, he rattled on about the history of the place—how it was a vast labyrinth of tunnels and chalk mines, some dating back to the time of the Druids. After a few minutes he led them into a wider area.

'This is going to be your hotel for the night.'

Fern's mouth dropped open. There were

'rooms' in the caves, cut out of the soft chalk, lined with low foam mattresses, each with a sleeping bag.

'We're going to sleep here?' she stammered.

'People have been using these caves for shelter for centuries—longer, probably,' their guide answered. 'During the Second World War, there was a thriving community down here. Come and see.'

He led them on a quick tour of the immediate area. She could hardly believe it. People had lived down here for weeks on end during the Blitz? There had been a cinema, a church, a dining hall—practically everything a person could need, all on hand in the safety of the caves.

'What a miserable existence,' Josh muttered as the guide led them back to their dormitory, one of three they'd discovered.

'Hardly miserable.' She gave him a curious look. 'A little damp at times, maybe, but it could have been nice. They must have had a terrific sense of community, of pulling together.'

He walked to the end of the low room and back again. 'I couldn't do it, not even if I'd lived back then. It's like being trapped. I'd have preferred to have been above the ground and run for the nearest shelter when the siren sounded.' He shook his head. 'No, this isn't living—it's hiding.'

Fern sat down on a mattress, happy to take the weight off her aching feet. 'I hardly think it's cowardly to want to keep safe, to keep the people you love safe. It seems like common sense to me.'

He flopped on to the mattress beside her. 'I'd rather live.'

Fern wrinkled her nose. That was the point, surely? Being in the caves would have ensured that people didn't get killed.

The evening wore on and more teams started to appear. Predictably, Kate and Aidan were the next to arrive and chose a pair of mattresses on the far side of the room from Josh and Fern, keeping an eye on them.

The treasure hunt organisers provided a meal of soup and sandwiches, which Fern devoured so quickly she surprised herself. By ten o'clock she was yawning so hard and so frequently that when Josh patted her sleeping bag and gave her a knowing look, she didn't put up a fight.

She was so tired her head was swimming but, even so, when she lay down inside the sleeping bag and closed her eyes, she couldn't fall asleep properly. All she could hear echoing in her ears were Josh's words from earlier: 'I'd rather live.'

And, as she tossed and turned, the images of a past she could only imagine roamed through her mind. Women with neatly curled hair and gravy browning on their legs instead of stockings. Children in grey clothes with gas masks in boxes looped round their necks on string.

Living down here in the darkness must have been strange. It would have become its own little world, with its share of triumphs, gossip and bickering. The horror of the outside would eventually have melted away, gone blurry and out of focus.

And what surprised her the most while she was thinking this was the fact that, until this week, she had been living that way. Hiding.

Her life was a safe little bubble. Boring sometimes, but always safe, always predictable. From the moment Ryan had died, her parents had made sure it stayed that way. As a child, and even more as a teenager, they'd lectured her on everything—how to cross the road, what to eat, her health.

She'd always thought she'd cut the apron strings from her parents, had moved on and become her own person, but now she'd stepped outside her life for a day and stood looking back at it, she realised that everything she did was about maintaining the status quo. Along the way, she'd soaked up more of her parents' mind-numbing lectures than she'd realised.

Today had been different. Just one day and she had a whole new perspective on things. Today she had *lived*.

She rolled over and looked at Josh in the semi-darkness. Now the lights had been turned down low, she could see the outline of him as he lay on his back, legs crossed, hands tucked behind his head so his elbows stuck out.

Because of this man, today she'd felt more fear, anxiety, desire and joy than she'd felt in weeks. Years, even. Yes, sometimes she'd been uncomfortable. Yes, she'd raged and sulked, but she'd also cheered and punched the air at times. And even the negative experiences had provoked a reaction in her that had let her know she was a living, breathing human being.

She sighed. What a difference from the usual coma of her life.

'Can't sleep?' Josh's voice was low, only a soft rumble.

She shook her head, even though he probably

couldn't see her. 'No,' she whispered. She longed to inch closer to him, to curl against his long frame and feel his warmth.

She must have sent out a subliminal message because, a few seconds later, he shuffled towards her, still on his back, and she could feel the warmth of his leg and side against her, even through the thickness of two sleeping bags. She inched just a little closer, holding her breath, then let it all out and relaxed against him.

'How's your new house?' she asked, not wanting to close her eyes just yet and let sleep blot out this lovely warm feeling that was creeping up on her. 'You were just about to exchange contracts last time I saw you.'

'It's fine.'

In the dark, Fern rolled her eyes. 'I'm a girl, Josh. I need more detail than that. What's the décor like?'

He groaned. 'I bet you're not going to let me go to sleep until I tell you, are you?'

'Yes, you are absolutely right about that.'

'Actually, there's a bit of a funny story attached to it. A year after I got the keys I was still partially living out of boxes with the furniture from my old flat filling about a quarter of the space.'

She could imagine that. Pauline Adams had shown her the estate agent's brochure. Not a grainy sheet of photocopied paper—a *brochure*, if you don't mind. It was one of those tall white houses in Notting Hill that seemed to be the average family home in Hollywood films. In reality, it would leave a dent of several million in the bank account.

'What happened?'

'Mum started to nag me about the state of the place. Apparently, having bare floorboards and no curtains at the windows after all that time was disgraceful. But I just hadn't had time to unpack and think about what I wanted to do with it.'

Fern's eyes grew large. 'In a whole year you didn't have time to unpack?'

She could feel the slight shake of his head against her shoulder. 'Not really. I was only ever there a few days at a time between trips.'

Fern smiled. No way would Pauline have let that one lie. 'What did she do?'

'In the end, she nagged me into hiring an interior designer. Then I went to New Zealand and I forgot all about it. Came back a month later at three in the morning, didn't bother turning the lights on and was scared half to death by one of my own African masks hanging in the hallway.'

Fern giggled. That, she would have paid money to see.

A comfortable silence fell. Even though their lives were so very different, they could still find some common ground. They both had strong-minded mothers who stuck their noses a little too deep into their children's lives. Money didn't make any difference to things like that.

'What are the neighbours like?' she said, thinking of the slightly annoying guy in the flat below hers. Everyone had stories about their neighbours.

'Loud, occasionally.'

She nodded. Downstairs guy had a passion for heavy metal she was praying he'd be cured of shortly. 'Have you met them?'

'Only in passing.' He mentioned the name of a well-known American rock singer and her British film star husband. 'He likes gardening, would you believe? Grows his own herbs. Offered me some basil for a pasta sauce once.'

She closed her eyes. Similar lives? Yeah, right. She lived upstairs from an unwashed computer geek and he lived next door to the bright young things of London and Hollywood. And Josh had probably been smooth and charming and had fitted right in without a second thought.

Her heartbeat was soft in her ears as she lay still and listened to the sound of her breathing—which was completely out of synch with Josh's. When she inhaled, he exhaled, and vice versa. Even if she tried to fall into rhythm with him she couldn't.

How short-sighted she'd been to think that lack of physical proximity had been their obstacle. When he'd moved out and gone to university their lives had diverged. For a while they'd been like trains on the same track, then someone had pulled a switch and the points had changed, and he'd headed off in one direction while she'd gone in another. Now she felt like the serviceable freight train to his Orient Express.

She was tucked up against him, closer than they'd been in years, but never had the distance between them been so vast.

CHAPTER SIX

Twelve years earlier

FERN peeped into the crowded church hall and then turned to sink against the wall of the corridor, her back against the cool plaster. She closed her eyes and breathed out a silent prayer of thanks.

He'd made it.

Josh was here and, although he'd promised he would be, she hadn't known whether to believe it or not. Last week he'd been in Turkey and the month before that, Madagascar. It had seemed at times that his gap year would never end and that he'd never come home to go to university.

As she relaxed a bit further against the wall, the netting in the petticoat of her party dress made a crunchy noise and scratched the back of her legs. Almost automatically, she tugged the strapless bodice into place by digging her thumbs under the edge and pulling upwards.

She heaved herself upright and took another look inside the church hall. Her party was in full swing, all her friends from school and the youth group dancing the night away. He was over there—talking to the DJ. Her stomach turned icy and rolled over. And then, as if he sensed her looking at him, sensed the connection, he lifted his head and smiled. She tried to remember to be sophisticated, to pull herself tall and be elegant, but the urge to flop into a heap was practically irresistible. She forced herself to take a few more steps into the room.

The heels on her shoes weren't too high, just a couple of inches, but for some unknown reason her ankle buckled slightly and the graceful, poised walk she'd practised for weeks became an ungainly stumble. She glared at her treacherous ankles and when she looked up again he was gone.

Just as she was considering backing up a bit and returning to the safety of the corridor, she felt a hand slide into hers. The melting, rushing, tingling feeling skipping up her arm told her who it was.

'Come on, birthday girl. You've danced with everyone but me.'

Without waiting for an answer, he did a little pull and a twist as he tugged her hand and she found herself turning, the skirt of her knee-length dress flaring out, then dropping back against her thighs as she came to a stop in his arms.

Oh, my. How many times had she dreamed about this moment? Hundreds? Thousands, probably. But in her dreams she'd always known what to do, what to say. She felt her cheeks heat and looked away. Don't blow this.

The music was fairly up-tempo and, thanks to Josh, she didn't stay still for long. He spun her away and back to him, turned her around, even dipped her, and she found herself laughing and joining in, forgetting that her feet normally turned to blocks of wood whenever she got within sight of a dance floor.

When the track ended, she fanned herself with her hand.

'You should go outside,' he suggested. 'Cool off a bit.'

She stammered. It very well might be nice and cool in the little garden adjoining the church hall, but it was away from Josh and that was the last place she wanted to be. He was slipping away, just as he did in those awful moments when she was ripped from her dreams by the grey morning light.

Josh was already leading her to the French

windows that led on to the patio next to the hall. He opened the door for her and she walked through it. What else could she do? Say, *Stay, kiss me?* She didn't have the courage. She walked over to a silver birch and placed her hand on its silky bark.

So, the moment she'd been waiting for had come…and gone.

A sigh escaped her lips and her shoulders drooped. Sixteen had seemed a magical age to her before she'd arrived here. The point at which she would no longer be a child, but a woman. The point at which he'd open his eyes and *see* her. Only he hadn't seen her at all. She was still little Fern, the kid next door who got a pity dance on her birthday. She closed her eyes to stop the stinging.

The plastic cup was so full that its contents were already dripping randomly on Josh's shoes. He paused at the threshold and stared out into the night. Where had she gone?

He stepped out into the garden and noticed a pale shadow further down the lawn. It was Fern, standing by the birch tree, the pale blonde of her swept-up hair and the creamy skin of her bare shoulders reflecting the soft moonlight. Something tugged inside him. Something warm and raw. Something he'd never expected to feel—and certainly shouldn't feel—when he looked at Fern.

Heck, if Ryan had been alive today, and had known he'd been feeling *this way* about his baby sister, he'd have punched Josh's lights out. And he'd have deserved it too.

He was almost at the birch now and she turned, hearing his footsteps on the grass. Her face registered surprise.

'I brought you a drink. You looked thirsty,' he said, suddenly finding his mouth dry too.

She looked incredible. I mean, that dress. When had Fern started to look like that—going in and out, all soft curves—and why hadn't he noticed it before?

Twin desires raged within him. His knight-in-shining-armour self was coming under attack from his teenage hormones. And, well, being not quite twenty, he was horribly afraid that the hormones were winning.

She smiled at him gently. 'Thank you.'

As she took the glass from him, their fingers brushed. It made him tingle in places he didn't want to tingle. Blood began to rush round his whole body. He could see enough in the glow of the light from the party that her pupils were wide and black and he knew instinctively that her heart was racing just as fast and hard as his was. The cool night air began to crackle.

'How have you been enjoying your party?' Odd, how his voice had become unusually scratchy at the end of that sentence. He'd just been watching her lips as she'd taken a sip of the fruit cocktail he'd handed her and, all of a sudden, his vocal cords had gone tight.

She stopped drinking and leaned back against the tree trunk. Her skirt billowed forward as she pressed one hand behind her back and one shoulder jutted forward, emphasising the elegant curve of her neck. She lowered her lashes and took another sip of her drink. He felt heat rush from his feet right to the roots of his hair.

Quick! Get back inside before you do something stupid.

He shifted his weight on to his back foot and prepared to turn away.

'I wish Ryan could have been here. I miss him.' Her voice was quiet and soft, with a hint of unshed tears. He'd be the biggest rat in the world if he left her out here alone now.

She finished her drink, placed the cup on the

ground and let out a ragged sigh. He didn't need to see her properly to know that her eyes were shimmering and that tiny beads of moisture were travelling down her cheeks.

He looked briefly back at the flashing lights of the disco inside the hall. So close, and yet so far. He really had no choice. He stepped forward and ran a hand down her arm. Then, knowing it wasn't enough, softly drew her into a hug. She came into his arms silently and he felt her ribcage shudder beneath his fingers.

This was better. He was her guardian again now, her protector. Things were shifting back on to an even keel. Only, as she relaxed against him, nestled her head against his shoulder, things began to go wrong. He realised that he very badly wanted to kiss her, wanted to reach across and tip her face upwards so he could taste those ripe pink lips.

His hormones were staging a coup and he was powerless to stop them. Fern moved and he caught a waft of her fresh floral perfume as she raised her head to look at him. Her eyes were wide and glistening. She was so fresh, so pretty. He knew he shouldn't, but he just couldn't stop himself. His gaze drifted down to her lips again.

Big mistake.

Magnetically, he was drawn to them, closer and closer until skin met skin, warm and pliant. She tasted so good, of sweet fruit punch and something more. Heaven help him, he couldn't prevent himself from exploring those lips. At first he was only aware of the slight hesitant response, but after a few seconds she began to kiss him back and he held her tighter and pressed her back against the bark of the tree, exploring the skin of her face, neck and shoulders with the tips of his fingers. Never had he imagined that sweet, fragile little Fern could ignite such a fire within him.

He felt her breath catch rather than heard it and she wound her arms around his neck, her fingers teasing the short hairs at the nape of his neck.

The fire that had been slowly spreading in him turned into an inferno. Suddenly, he knew he wanted to do a lot more than just *kiss* sweet, innocent Fern, and the thought scared the hell out of him.

She was too young—way too young—and he was due at university in only a month. He couldn't offer her what she wanted. It wasn't fair to even try.

He gently cupped her face in his hands and pulled away, even though every cell in his body protested. As she came into focus, he saw her eyelids flutter open and knew from the look in her eyes that if he went further down this road she was going to fall for him. Hard.

It was there in the sweet sparkle of hope in her eyes. A tiny part of him leapt for joy, but he squashed it down fiercely. What a blind idiot he'd been not to recognise it before. She had a crush on him. Had done for years. Before now he'd never been able to put a name to that blush, that sparkle, until it had intensified to the level it was tonight and he'd recognised it for what it was.

Stupid, stupid, stupid.

He stepped back but held on to her hand. Now was the time to be really, really careful. He had to let her down gently; she was way too special to play with.

He tried to smile naturally and hoped he didn't look as tense and awkward as he felt. 'Fern,' he began, then looked away briefly before connecting his gaze with hers again. 'We need to talk.'

She woke up with a start, her breath coming in gasps. She didn't sit up, too scared of waking

Josh, who was curled behind her. He'd ask questions. He'd want to know why she was crying.

Damn. She swept away the tears with an angry hand and tried to regulate the rhythm of her lungs. It was that stupid dream. Every now and then she'd have it and be transported back to that toe-curlingly embarrassing moment. The party. That stupid dress. Her own foolish teenage expectations.

She'd offered herself to Josh on a plate and he'd said, Thanks, but no, thanks, and walked off to university, never once looking back. It had been more than a decade ago and, in her waking life, nothing more than something to chalk up to experience, make a note of and move on. But, somehow, her subconscious just wasn't willing to let it go.

She exhaled and made the breath last for a count of ten. Her heart rate was slowing now, but the emotions of the dream were still pulsating in the air around her, making her feel as raw as a jilted sixteen-year-old.

Let's think about this logically. She was probably only having the dream because she was spending time with Josh. Something had pushed some long-forgotten emotional buttons.

Her arm was going numb and she shifted on to her other side, only to discover she was almost nose to nose with him. She shuffled again so her back was in contact with the mattress and stared at the long shadows on the rough-lit ceiling. He stirred and she held her breath, not ready for him to wake up yet. She needed time to sort out the tangled mess of her thoughts before she looked into those melting brown eyes.

She'd been half kidding herself, hadn't she? Half pretending that there was a little bit of chemistry flitting between her and Josh, when in reality she knew that it was totally a one-way street. And she still had more than two days to go, being in his company every waking moment. Great plan, Fern! That will really help you move on.

Suddenly, something clicked inside her. Maybe it could be good. Maybe this was the perfect way to get some closure. By the time the treasure hunt finished, she might have found a way to shift the relationship back on to an entirely platonic track, back to when she'd been—she grimaced in the dark—about nine years old. Crumbs, had she really been infatuated with him for that long? Maybe even that was being optimistic. She'd had a severe case of hero worship even before that.

No, the next couple of days were going to be about finding a *new* foundation for her relationship with Josh. One where they were both adults. Equals. Where one of them was definitely over the hormone-induced roller coaster of teenage crushes. And it was about time she bucked her ideas up. In the last twenty-four hours she'd been guilty of letting her guard down, allowing him to get to her again.

Maybe the dream had been a timely warning from her subconscious. Don't go there. Keep off. Danger.

It was time to build the barriers back up—defences so solid and sure that even a pair of warm chocolate eyes with a hint of *zap* couldn't melt them.

Suddenly everything went dark. Fern gingerly pressed her fingertips to the outside of the blindfold that now covered her eyes.

Now her vision was reduced to nothing, the damp, dark smell of the caves intensified. She could hear Josh grinning beside her as his own blindfold was fixed in place. Don't ask her *how* she could hear something like that; she just could.

'This way.'

The treasure hunt marshal must have taken hold of Josh's hand, because the fingers that threaded themselves through hers were definitely his. She gripped on to them as they started to move and flung her other arm wide in an attempt to find the moist, rough chalk wall to her left.

As the guide led them through the network of caves to the starting point for the next leg of the treasure hunt, she tried to memorise the directions and number of turns they took, paying attention to the points where her fingers drifted past nothing but cold air, indicating the presence of another passage.

It wasn't easy to concentrate. Each of the remaining thirty teams were being led to exactly the same destination, five at a time, and the noise of footsteps, stumbles and not-too-hushed swearing threatened to dislodge the sequence of directions carefully ordered in her short-term memory.

She tried to remember specific places—anchor points—certain turns in the route, changes in the texture of the floor under her trainers. Josh started whistling and she gave a frustrated tug on his arm to shut him up. It was not helping.

After a short while all the teams were assembled in a section of damp corridor. A treasure hunt marshal hushed them and spoke loudly above the lingering whispers. 'The first ten teams to arrive last night will start first and, fifteen minutes behind them, the next ten teams, and so on. You will all be receiving a map of the caves shortly—' Fern heard the rustle of paper as someone else walked along the row and she thrust out her hand to grab a sheet. 'When you hear the first whistle, the first group of teams must remove their blindfolds and navigate their way back to the entrance, where they will find the next clue. Is everybody clear?'

There was a general murmuring and Fern nodded, aware that her heart-rate had just skipped up a notch. She was just about to take a deep preparatory breath when the whistle blew. She gulped the air in quickly and her fingers worked at the knot behind her head. Once it had loosened, she slipped it backwards over her head and stared at the map, blinking rapidly. Shapes and lines danced in front of her eyes and settled into more regular patterns. It was impossible to work out where they were on the map. All the square tunnels looked the same. They needed to find a feature—an unusual intersection or a dead end—to help them get their bearings.

Josh let go of her hand to deal with his blindfold. 'What do you reckon?' he asked, pausing to glance sideways as a couple of other teams dashed off in different directions.

She looked long and hard at an opening to their left, sure they'd been led to this section of tunnel from that direction. It was all Josh needed. Within seconds he was running and she followed him, warm with the knowledge that he trusted her—trusted her instincts.

Almost immediately, they came to another intersection. She worked back through the series of memorised directions in her head. The turn before that one had been a right turn, so they would have to go…

'Left,' she said and they were off again. They continued in a similar manner for a few minutes and she felt her confidence growing. Every now and then she would shut her eyes and silently mouth the memorised sequence before heading off in a new direction.

'Have you noticed something?' She kept her voice low, wary of being overheard for some reason.

Josh stopped jogging and turned to face her. 'What?'

'When we first started going we kept bumping into the other teams. We haven't seen anyone else for a couple of minutes.' She felt her smile spreading her lips even as she spoke. 'That could mean we've maintained our lead and—'

They both stopped running. Twenty people, all wearing red T-shirts and blindfolds blocked their way. She and Josh were right back where they'd started. Somewhere along the line she must have got confused. She looked in desperation at Josh.

'Never mind.' He tugged her back in the direction they'd taken the first time.

'But that isn't the right way!'

'It was one wrong turn, Fern. I think you were right up to a point, but a couple of wrong choices near the end got us confused.'

She jogged behind Josh as he retraced their steps and scanned the map to see where she'd gone wrong. There had been one point where she hadn't been quite sure…

When they reached the same spot again, she stopped to consider the options: left, right or straight on. Josh only took a second to make up his mind and headed left.

'Josh! Wait! What are you doing?'

'I'm going this way. I've got a feeling.'

'No!' That was the way they'd gone last time. They'd be going in circles if they repeated their earlier decision.

'Go with the flow, Fern.'

She chewed her lip for a moment. 'Okay. If we are going to flow anywhere, then let's *flow* this way.' She pointed in the opposite direction. The floor of the cave was harder there, like petrified ripples of sand. She was sure she'd felt some of that beneath her rubber soles when she'd been blindfolded.

However, a few minutes later she heard a whistle blow in an adjoining passageway and suddenly they had to press themselves against the wall to avoid being mown down by the second group of teams as they fanned out, looking for the exit. Back to the start *again*?

Adrenaline surged through her. And not in a good way. Her brain pounded against her skull and the list of directions stored there was jostled out of order.

Josh gave her a rueful grin. 'Third time lucky.' He shrugged, then set off the way they'd gone twice before. Fern slapped her forehead with her palm and, without stopping to let herself feel it stinging, she ran after him.

This time, when they reached the infernal crossroads again, Josh didn't hesitate, he went left and she had no choice but to follow him.

'Trust me,' he yelled, without looking back. 'I've got a feeling.'

Yes, well, *feelings* were all well and good when you didn't have treasure to find. *Feelings* weren't going to get them out of these caves. *Feelings* were generally getting her into trouble at the moment. What they needed were cold, hard facts. Something to tie them firmly to the ground.

Josh didn't slow his pace for the next few moments and it was all she could do to keep up with him. Then, suddenly, the air grew sweeter, cleaner, and the honeycomb of identical tunnels opened out into the large area they'd used as a dining room last night.

It had worked! Somehow Josh's *feeling* had led them to the entrance of the caves.

She frowned as they reached the small table near the ticket office with the next clues laid out on it. A quick count revealed only fifteen left. That meant they'd lost their lead completely and were now halfway down the pack.

Josh kneaded her shoulders while she tore open the envelope.

'What can I say?' he said. 'Sometimes you've just got to trust your instincts.'

'No! No way.' Fern shook her head and planted her hands firmly on her hips.

'You can't say *no*!'

Fern's ponytail was still swinging gently from side to side, an echo of her vehement refusal. This was probably not a good sign, Josh decided.

'You're not really going to back out now, are you?'

'Yes?'

There was a glint of regret in her eyes and he knew he was in with a chance of making her change her mind. She dropped her backpack on to the cobblestone pavement and sat on top of it.

He could hardly believe this was the same woman that he'd seen dive off a crane less than forty-eight hours ago. He thought there'd been a dramatic change in her when he'd spotted her ready to bungee jump, but she hadn't changed, not really. She was still the same sensible Fern she'd always been. Then he had a memory flash—Fern clinging to a narrow plank walkway in an adventure playground fifteen feet above the muddy floor, terrified out of her wits but determined to prove to Ryan that she wasn't a scaredy cat.

Back then, aged twelve, he'd laughed and called her chicken. Well, twelve-year-old boys weren't known for their ability to empathise, were they? Back then, he hadn't understood how hard it had been for her, trailing round after two boys who knew no fear. He'd walked that plank hundreds of times, never giving it a second thought.

But now he looked back over the years and realised she'd always had that brave, determined streak. And it was why he'd made time for Ryan's supposedly 'annoying' little sister. If he thought about it hard, he might have to admit that she had more guts than he did. Flinging himself off the top of high things or swirling through white-water rapids came easily to him. The bottom line was he just wasn't scared. But Fern…

A noise that was half whimper, half sigh escaped from the hunched up figure beside him. He smiled, not at pleasure from her inner torment, but because he knew she was going to do it. Because that was the kind of woman she was.

Woman. He didn't think he'd mentally applied that word to her before. He'd always vaguely labelled her as a 'girl'. But it'd been a long while since they'd spent any kind of quality time together, years even. And he was starting to see all sorts of things about Fern that he'd been blind to before.

Fern tightened her already dissolving ponytail with a quick tug, then stood up. 'Okay, let's get the show on the road. What are we going to do?'

'I could juggle. That worked quite well yesterday.'

Fern shook her head. Josh's haphazard juggling skills weren't going to help in this challenge. They were standing in Covent Garden, one of London's hippest places to hang out in the summer. The old market square was filled to the brim with coffee shops, restaurants and fashionable boutiques.

The clue they'd got at the caves had instructed them to perform a task. Once again they had to earn money to help them fund their way through the race. And this time the organisers were upping the stakes.

Today they had to—not sing for their supper—but busk for their breakfast. Although it was early, there were already a number of street artists working the crowd. On the other side of the square a man dressed head to toe in silver juggled kitchen knives and flaming torches. No, Josh's fruit tricks definitely weren't going to cut the mustard here.

When she turned to him, he was looking over in the same direction. He nodded despondently. 'We're going to have to sing, aren't we?'

'Sing?' Her voice came out all scratchy and high. 'With no music or anything?'

'What else can we do?'

'But neither of us can hold a tune. My family even actively ban me from joining in with the carols at Christmas because I murder them.'

He looked at her and gave her a slow smile that melted her insides. 'There is that.'

She scanned the area and noticed a few other red Secret London T-shirts scattered throughout the market square. 'What do you think the other teams are going to do?'

Abruptly, he ruffled her hair in a non-melting-inside kind of way. It was a gesture more akin to the Chinese burns he'd inflicted on her when they'd been children. The warm, fizzy feeling that had been growing inside her packed its bags and left.

'I've got it! Wait here.'

Before she could answer, he raced off across the square in the direction of one of the other teams. She squinted in the low-slanting morning sun. Was it the twin brothers he was talking to? Moments later, they were all racing back to where she was standing near the portico of St Paul's Church.

'How much money have you got?' Josh said to them all as they drew to a halt. They all fumbled around in their pockets and pulled out a few notes and some change. Josh took some from the twins and from Fern, then sprinted off across the square again.

What on earth was he doing? As she followed his path, she realised he was heading straight for a flower stall. Please, please, let him not be planning to juggle carnations! It would be too humiliating.

She exchanged nervous smiles with the twins, whose names she had been told yesterday, but had forgotten. Her feet itched and she jigged from one to the other while she waited to see what Josh was going to do. When the florist picked up a whole armful of carnations, her heart sank. But then, as she stood gaping, Josh handed the florist the money, picked up the big black bucket the flowers had been sitting in and tipped all the water out over the cobblestones. When he'd repeated the process a couple more times, he returned with four buckets of assorted sizes. By this time the twins were grinning.

'I reckon,' Josh said as he handed the twins the buckets, 'that if we join forces on this one, we'll all benefit.'

The twins looked at each other and nodded.

'Fern? Is that okay with you?'

Everyone looked at her. She swallowed. 'Yes.'

'Do you want to warm up a bit, boys?'

The *boys* immediately dumped the buckets upside down on the floor and used their backpacks as makeshift stools. They began thumping the bases of the buckets and repositioning them every few seconds until they were happy with the sounds they were making.

Josh whispered in her ear, 'I got chatting to Sam and Rob after dinner last night and the conversation turned to music. They play in a band. Just a hobby, but last night Rob was messing around with the cups and glasses, playing them with his fork and spoon, and he was pretty good. Then when you said something about the "other teams" it gave me an idea.'

Fern raised an eyebrow. 'Am I going to like this idea?'

'It has to be better than singing *a cappella*. Listen.'

The twins started tapping on the bases of the

upturned buckets, using them as bongos. Sam set up a steady rhythm, then Rob began to do some more fancy syncopated arrangements over the top. Actually, it sounded pretty good. Kind of Cuban. Her feet started moving of their own accord, her hips swaying. She began to smile.

She turned to find Josh staring at her.

'What?'

'I think I've just had an even better idea than singing.'

He had a look in his eyes that made her feel distinctly giddy. He moved towards her and she backed away, but he kept on coming. Sometimes, when Josh really wanted something, he got very serious and his normal easygoing manner vanished. It was exactly that masculine intensity that had first made her heart flutter for him. As it was, her pulse was now skipping along way too fast to match the twins' laid-back Latin percussion.

His fingers closed around hers and he held on to them firmly. She stared back at him, too full of all sorts of tingly feelings to get any words out. He looked as if he wanted to eat her whole.

Was he going to kiss her now? Right here in the middle of Covent Garden?

CHAPTER SEVEN

FERN knew she ought to back away, but part of her still went gooey at the thought. And, unfortunately, that part seemed to have control of her legs at this particular moment. One of Josh's hands slid along her arm until it reached her elbow and the fingers of his other hand interlaced with hers. Just as she was about to sway towards him, lips at the ready, he started to move, his feet stepping in a backwards-and-forwards pattern she recognised.

Without her asking them to, her legs joined in. Where he led, she followed. She glanced down at their feet, mirror images of each other, then back up at him. He grinned.

'We're salsa dancing,' she said in an incredulous voice.

'Sure looks like it,' he replied as he smoothly let her out of the basic back-and-forwards step she'd learned only a few days before into a side-step.

'I can't salsa! Not properly.'

He raised an eyebrow, then changed his arm positions to lead her across the front of his body so they switched places, all the time keeping up the same rhythm with his feet. 'Um, I hate to tell you this, Fern, but I think you already are.'

Well, yes, she knew a few of the basic steps, but it was hardly more than that. Even though the music was conducive to swaying and wiggling, her legs were stiff and awkward. She was terrified that she'd fall out of rhythm and then—even worse—fall over altogether.

'You know what I mean,' she whispered.

Josh just shrugged and spun her out to one side, only to bring her back again. 'You were doing fine just a moment ago when Rob and Sam started playing.'

She frowned. 'That was different. I…'

'Didn't think you were being watched? What does it matter?'

It mattered because she was bound to make a fool of herself, in front of the handful of people who had stopped strolling and were now looking in their direction and, more importantly, in front of him. She gaped and her mouth worked while she tried to find a good excuse. She certainly wasn't going to tell him the truth.

He had that sexy, serious look in his eyes again. The half dozen words she had queuing up in her mind for the start of her next sentence all switched places. His voice was low and sensual when he said, 'Close your eyes.'

She did as she was told, not able to handle being looked at like that for another second anyway. It was doing strange things to her nervous system. Breathing no longer seemed to be automatic.

Even more than before, she was reliant on him to guide her. He kept the steps basic, alternating between the forward-and-backward step and the side-to-side combinations she knew.

'When did you learn to salsa, Josh Adams?'

His low chuckle reverberated right through her. 'You can't visit South America as often as I have without picking up some of this stuff.'

She held her breath suddenly as, with a lean of his body and a flick of his wrist, he propelled her into an underarm turn. Her eyes popped open as she came to rest back in his arms, closer than before. Oh, boy, she needed more oxygen. Badly.

The echoes of his laughter died away, leaving

only a thick silence behind. They were looking deep into each other's eyes now, joined by more than hands and arms, by more than quick swaying steps that kept them locked in rhythm with each other. Her muscles relaxed and she melted into the movements, finding she was no longer just being led and positioned by him, but that she was letting the music seep into her bones.

Now they were working together, Josh tried more complicated moves and Fern found herself flowing through them as easily as if she'd been doing it for years. As long as she relaxed, kept the right rhythm going with her feet, it all seemed to come together.

Pretty soon she was smiling back at him, adding a few little flicks of her feet, a few extra wiggles of her hips, just like she'd seen the more advanced dancers do at her class.

Vaguely, somewhere in the distance, she heard a ripple of applause, the chink of coins dropping into an empty plastic bucket, but she kept her eyes locked on Josh's.

Braver, she tried something she'd seen Lisette do when they'd been out dancing. She raised her arms above her head, then, after a few beats, ran her fingers through her hair, pulling the band out of her ragged ponytail as she did so, then smoothed her hands down the sides of her torso, ending somewhere near her hips. Josh made a spluttering noise and she looked sharply at him.

'What's wrong?'

He swallowed and, just for a split second, lost his footing. 'Nothing. Nothing at all. In fact, I'd say you were a real natural at this.'

She smiled back at him, the momentary tension drifting away. 'I'm not doing too bad, am I? Who would have known?'

Josh coughed and looked at the ground. 'Yeah,' he muttered. 'Who would?'

The twins changed the tempo slightly, speeding up, and both Fern and Josh had to concentrate for a few bars. The smiles on their faces vanished and her breathing became rapid, her heart rate steady but pulsing in her veins.

Once they'd adjusted to the new speed, they broke out of the basic steps again. Josh was turning her almost constantly now and, amazingly, she was keeping up. He was right. When she just let it all flow through her she ended up going the right way, doing the right thing, without even thinking about it.

'Nearly there,' she heard one of the twins call between thumps on the buckets.

Josh's eyes simmered. 'Time for the finale,' he whispered and flicked her this way and that. Then, just as she thought she'd experienced everything in his repertoire, he sprang a new move on her.

As they rocked in a basic step, backwards and forwards, he let both his hands slide down her arms so he was holding her hands. Then he moved her arms up and over and his fingertips brushed along the length of her arms and ended up on the back of her shoulders. Her hands came naturally to rest on his chest.

With his hands splayed on her shoulder blades, he swung her quickly side to side, then dipped her back, holding her so her legs were together and her back was arched right over. She gasped.

He pulled her up straight, so close they were almost glued together. Her blood began to simmer. There was only a hair's breadth between their bodies and, as their eyes met, their hips began to sway in unison. She fought the urge to close her eyes and sigh as Josh's hands ran down her back and cupped her bottom.

Seamlessly, he moved into the next step and his hands returned to the small of her waist before he dipped her back again, this time in a long, slow circular motion. She gave way to it completely, savouring the slow sexiness of it, feeling the play of her back muscles beneath his hands as he moved and supported her all at once.

This time, when they returned to standing, she made sure that she held on to his back to steady herself and, when he pulled her completely upright, one of her hands squeezed a taut buttock in reply. Josh's eyes widened.

'Tit for tat,' she whispered, amazed at her own boldness. A smile crept across his lips—a hungry male smile—and something inside her soared at the knowledge that it was sweet, innocent Fern who had put it there.

As the sights and sounds around them came back into focus, she realised that people were clapping and whistling. The twins were scooping coins out of the bucket—lots of coins.

The treasure hunt. The challenge. For a few minutes she'd forgotten all about them.

A sudden rush of cold hit her and travelled down to the pit of her stomach. She was standing in the middle of Covent Garden with a cheeky smile on her face and one hand on Josh's bottom. And, worse than that, she wasn't entirely sure she wanted to let go. What on earth did she think she was doing?

So much for re-erecting the defensive shield! What was she going to do now?

As gently as she could, she lifted her fingers away from the now-warm denim covering his backside and retreated. He cocked his head to one side and raised his eyebrows, still smiling.

'Looks like we've got enough,' she said, letting the words tumble out on a rushing breath. 'Time to move on.'

In the narrow tile-lined tunnel that ran under the River Thames, Josh could see another two teams in front of them. He nodded at Fern and they speeded up a little. For someone who was petite and slender, she was surprisingly fit.

Their footsteps echoed, bouncing off the smooth walls and making a slapping sound as each foot met with the concrete floor. Feeling the lactic acid burning in his muscles was good. It stole his attention away from other things he didn't want to think about—almost as effective as a cold shower.

He'd never even known of the existence of this Victorian pedestrian tunnel at Greenwich, the only clue to its presence two strange dome-like buildings on opposite sides of the river. Once upon a time the lifts had worked. Of course, for the Secret London Treasure Hunt that would have been too easy. If there were the same number on the other side, they faced a wide spiral staircase of more than three hundred steps when they reached the end of the tunnel. He glanced at his partner. He hoped she could make it; they'd been running all morning since they'd got the second clue and left Covent Garden.

They slowed down as they reached the bottom of the stairs and took a few deep breaths, hands on knees, before tackling them.

'You okay?' he asked.

She nodded. Her face was pink and blotchy and she looked totally adorable.

He set off up the stairs first before she had a chance to get in front of him. Hardly the gentlemanly thing to do, he knew, but the other option was three hundred steps at eye level with Fern's bottom, which could provoke ungentlemanly behaviour of an entirely different sort—especially after the recent salsa fiasco. He got a sudden burst of speed just thinking about it.

Rats! The whole wear-himself-out-so-he-wouldn't-think-about-her-like-that thing just wasn't working.

He'd thought he'd been past all of that, had got all the 'Fern is hot' feelings out of his system. After all, it had only been a rush of teenage hormones. Only, twelve years on, he seemed to be having a relapse.

When he'd returned from university, during his sporadic visits home, neither of them had ever mentioned the kiss, or even the birthday party it had taken place at. By tacit agreement they'd just decided to sweep it all under the carpet and forget about it. Ryan would have been very proud of him.

For a whole term after he'd started university, he'd paid not the slightest attention to the girls there, even though they'd been away from home for the first time and ready to prove they were all grown up. It had been Fern's fault. He hadn't been able to get that kiss out of his mind.

But, over the years, they'd managed to put it behind them, had managed to build a friendship. And he was still keeping his promise. He was still looking out for her—when he was in the country, of course.

He lost his footing on the stairs and Fern crashed into the back of him. He could feel her pressed against his lower back and her hands, instinctively raised to brace herself, met with his rear end. He squeezed his eyes shut tight and made his voice as light and jokey as he could manage.

'Hey, lady, don't touch what you can't afford. I've had to warn you about that once already today.'

'Sorry,' she mumbled behind him.

The safest thing to do was just start moving again, no matter how hard his quadriceps were screaming.

When they finally emerged from the squat dome on the south side of the river, they grinned at each other. Their destination was right in front of them—the Cutty Sark, a beautiful old tea clipper and local tourist attraction.

'Have you got the clue?' He wiped the sweat off his forehead with the back of his arm. Fern reached in the front pocket of her backpack and pulled out the carefully folded clue.

'It says we've got to find "the fearless maiden with blue eyes and blonde flowing tresses".'

He looked straight at her. Another one?

She was reading further down the clue. 'It says she was "the brave spirit whose true heart kept men safe". What does that mean?'

Josh shook his head. He didn't know the answer to the question, but he did it mainly to shake the images of a certain brave, true-hearted woman out of his head. Lust he could handle—well, eventually he'd get a grip on himself—but these thoughts were something altogether more scary.

'I suppose we just go inside and find out.'

They explored the top deck, climbing in and out of the thick woven ropes and rigging, then decided to hunt below. Two decks down, they found what they were looking for: a whole room full of figureheads, all different shapes and designs, some human, some not.

Fern stood in the middle of the deck, spun on the spot and let out a breathy whistle. 'These are exquisite! I mean, look at the craftsmanship.'

Josh did look. But not at the lumps of wood. He couldn't look at anything but Fern as her eyes shone and her quick mind ticked away. She stopped spinning.

'What are you smiling at? Do I have dust on my face or something?' She rubbed her nose with the heel of her hand in a gesture that reminded him of a six-year-old with pigtails. 'Come on. This "true-hearted woman" has to be in here somewhere.' She turned and ran to the other end of the deck and started inspecting each carving in turn.

'Yes,' he agreed hoarsely. 'Yes, she must be.'

It seemed that Fern had always had the ability to surprise him, but he was starting to think that this was due to his own blindness rather than any significant change in her. For example, he'd always known she'd had a good sense of humour, but he hadn't known how cheeky, how *grown-up* she could be. It fascinated him. What else had he missed about her?

'Josh! Will you stop standing there like a lemon and *do* something?'

He grinned back at her. Yeah, he hadn't reckoned on that bossy streak, but he kind of liked it. 'Yes, ma'am.'

He walked to the nearest figurehead and took a look. It was a bust of Benjamin Disraeli, so he was pretty sure he hadn't struck gold yet. He moved on to the next chunk of wood.

His lack of insight probably had everything to do with the fact that he had been away so much. In his mind, Fern was still the same twenty-year-old who had greeted him softly and calmly at his graduation party. In the same way, until the night of her sixteenth birthday, she'd been the six-year-old with pigtails.

He'd promised to keep an eye out for her and, in his mind, he'd done that, even if it had been a bit long-distance recently. An image of his mother and father popped into his mind, the sad look in their eyes every time he left for the airport. He didn't stay put much. Life was easier that way. Only he was starting to realise that life was easier for *him* that way. Commitment was a lot more comfortable at a safe distance.

Fern and Josh skidded into the vast marble-floored entrance hall of the Victoria & Albert Museum only to find six other teams crowded round a treasure hunt marshall, pieces of paper waving in their hands. Almost all the teams were talking at the tops of their voices—apart from one couple who were just scratching their heads.

'What is the marshall handing out?' Fern asked, trying to find an opening in the group. 'Is it the map?' She looked down at the red clue clutched in her hand.

'It says we have to find a copy of Henry Beck's map. What kind of map?'

Josh wiggled his way further into the crowd, got a sheet of paper from the marshall, then edged his way out again. 'It says it's a map of the Underground. The original is in the print library here.'

She smiled, She'd been commuting for the last ten years and knew the tube network like the back of her hand. This clue was going to be as easy as pie to solve.

His brow furrowed as he turned the page round for her to get a proper look. '*Map* is rather a loose definition. It's a copy of a line drawing on a scrap of paper.'

Ten minutes later they were sitting in the café, wolfing down paninis in an effort to stay well-fuelled and puzzling over the photocopy of the 'map'. For the purpose of the treasure hunt, printed numbers had been added next to various blobs on the drawing.

'This isn't really a proper map, is it? It was just a sketch—his original idea to show the stations in relation to each other rather than on a geographical scale.'

Josh nodded. 'Little more than a doodle. These blobs on some of the lines must be stations. I'm guessing we'll have to work out which stations are numbered and visit them, taking pictures, in numerical order. One slip-up, one station wrong, and we're out of the race.'

She swallowed a mouthful of mozzarella, tomato and basil panini. 'That sounds logical.

Only—' she smoothed out the pocket tube map she'd picked up at Charing Cross on the table next to her '—it doesn't look much like this, does it?'

She squinted at Beck's doodle, hoping the roughly drawn lines would make a bit more sense if they were slightly out of focus. It was no good. Even blurry, the shapes bore little resemblance to the modern-day map.

Josh finished his panini and took a sip of cola. 'To be honest, yesterday was the first time I'd used the tube in years. I'm totally lost with this. I mean, I don't even remember the map being the way it is now. The circle line has changed shape and there are new extensions everywhere.'

Fern's bottle of mineral water was halfway to her mouth. She put it back on the table. 'I think you may have something there.'

She and Josh had been like this all day, sparking ideas off each other. Their team dynamic was perfect. They knew each other well enough to trust each other, to know where the other was going with a line of thought, but they were still able to stimulate each other, push each other to think outside the box.

Doing this treasure hunt was the single most

exciting thing she'd done in years. It was pushing her mentally and she was thriving on the challenge. What a pity it only lasted for four days; she could have kept going for weeks, months even.

Josh was bent over the map, his dark hair just within touching distance. It looked so thick and shiny. She tried very hard to block the next thought, the one whispering in the back of her head that, if Josh was by her side, she might be tempted to do this for ever.

His eyes flicked up and he caught her staring at him. She blushed.

'You were saying…?'

Um, yes, she was vaguely aware that she'd been talking, but for the life of her she couldn't remember what she'd been about to…

'I *had something*, remember?'

Once again, at Josh's stimulus, her brain woke up and began to whirr. She smiled at him. No one else did this to her—fired her up and made her feel as if she were zinging with life.

He drummed his fingers on the table.

'Oh, sorry! I was going to say that you were on to something about the map changing.' She prodded the unfolded pocket tube map on the table. 'If this simple diagram has changed within the last decade, think how different it must be from the first one produced in the Thirties.'

'We need to find the original printed map based on this design.'

'Exactly. Some stations must have closed and others must have been added. We need to find out what's still the same.'

They stood up in unison, letting their chairs scrape backwards, and leaving the remains of their lunch on the table. She'd just about finished anyway. Josh picked up his backpack.

'I think I saw something like that in the entrance—on a poster for an exhibition of Modernist design they're holding here this month. He must've been a bit of an original thinker, this Mr Beck.'

She swung her own bag on to her shoulders. 'Let's get going, then.'

'Thank goodness we had all that extra cash from the fruit and veg task,' Josh said as he handed over two ten pound notes to a uniformed woman and waited for change. 'The entry to the museum might be free, but they certainly make up for it by charging for the exhibitions.'

Fern shook her head. 'We were lucky, that's all.'

Josh took the tickets that the woman handed to him and they headed inside the exhibition. 'Just goes to show that sometimes taking a chance can reap bigger rewards than you'd ever expect.'

She grunted.

They found the big poster of the 1939 version of the Underground map easily and, thank goodness, this one was very similar to the pencil lines on the sketch. Once they'd located a few key points it was fairly easy to work out which stations the nameless blobs on the clue were.

The rest of the afternoon was spent racing other teams in and out of tube stations. All Josh's competitive juices were flowing at maximum levels. He'd had no idea his home town could be this exciting.

Fern was also as pumped up as he'd ever seen her. In fact, he could have sworn that before today he'd never seen her do 'excitable', but there she was, bouncing from foot to foot as the train sped through the dark tunnels, the tube map clenched in her fist.

'Two more stops,' she mouthed to him, then, louder, 'we need to move along a carriage. That way we'll be in exactly the right place to run straight off the train and into the exit for the

Metropolitan line.' She glanced over her shoulder quickly at a pair of red T-shirts further down the carriage and beckoned for him to come closer. 'That way we should beat those two to Moorgate.'

Fern's extensive knowledge of the tube network had been invaluable this afternoon, he thought, as at the next stop they jumped out and moved along one carriage. Her memory was amazing, practically photographic. He couldn't be one hundred per cent sure, but he guessed that they'd leap-frogged over enough teams to now be in the top five. Everything seemed to be going their way finally.

When the doors opened they were ready. They burst out of the train and ran straight into the exit tunnel for the Metropolitan line, just as Fern had predicted. They darted up a flight of stairs that led—after a journey through a minor labyrinth—to the next platform. A train was sitting there, its alarm pinging, warning that the doors were just about to close. They looked at each other and dived for the carriage, slipping inside just as there was a hissing noise and a rumble and the doors slid shut.

It was getting close to rush hour now and the carriages were getting progressively more crowded. This one, in the centre of the train, was full enough for them to be pressed against the doors. Fern wiggled round to see out of the window and giggled. 'Look!'

He turned too and found himself pressed up against her, front to front. Don't think about it, he warned himself, and looked where she was pointing. A chuckle burst out of his mouth. The team they'd been racing against were frantically banging on the illuminated button to make the door open, but it was too late. The engine whined and they moved forward with a jolt.

Heaven help him, the hormones were back. And this time he was pretty sure they'd come with reinforcements. He and Fern were fully clothed, for goodness' sake, and only just touching. She was pressed up against his chest and her scent was filling his nostrils. So close. He could see the wide blackness of her pupils and the faint colour in her cheeks.

If it wasn't his hormones, it was some strange genetic kick-back because, right at this moment, he felt almost compelled to drag her into his arms and make her his, like some caveman.

'Well, this is cosy.' He did his best to keep his voice low and nonchalant.

'Yes.' Fern took a deep breath and the heat in her cheeks increased. She knew without a doubt they'd just darkened to a rather obvious shade of pink.

To make matters worse, every time the train juddered on its rails they brushed against each other. There was no way she could ignore it. As her torso slid across his it detonated tiny electric shocks that made the hairs on the back of her neck stand on end. Every time she got close to imagining she was pressed up against something else—something neutral, like a cushion or a pillow—the train threw them off balance again and a whole rush of tingles travelled up her nerve endings to her brain, screaming all the way that it was Josh she was touching, Josh she was rubbing up against, Josh whose lips she could imagine brushing past her ear lobes, trailing down her neck…

Stop it! You are just making things worse for yourself.

On Monday morning she would be back in her stale old job, visiting the same old coffee shop for lunch and Josh would be gone. Their lives were so different that their paths only ever intersected briefly. Okay, he might stick around for a few weeks because of his dad, but eventually he'd be gone. He'd leave her behind again.

She turned to look out of the window. The only things visible were bunches of cables fixed to the wall of the tunnel, illuminated now and then by the bright lights of a passing train.

'So you do it every day, huh?'

This? What did he mean? And it sounded conspicuously as if he was making conversation. Since when had Josh resorted to small talk with her? She looked back at him quizzically, feeling the skin above her brows wrinkle.

'I don't think I could stand commuting,' he said.

Oh, of course. He was talking about taking the tube. For a minute there she hadn't the foggiest what he'd been going on about. Her normal life—her job, her parents, even Lisette and the dithering Simon—seemed like another life, one that had taken place on a far-away planet in another dimension.

He'd been back in her life for less than forty-eight hours, yet it was almost impossible to believe there'd be a time when Josh wouldn't be beside her, racing along crowded streets, skidding through quiet museum hallways. These few days, this treasure hunt, had become everything that mattered.

Nothing was real but the feeling of his hand in

hers as they raced from place to place, his smile when they cracked a clue, that intense way he looked at her sometimes, as if he were trying to look right through her. These were the things she lived and breathed for now. The treasure hunt had become its own little world, a bubble of super-charged life.

She closed her eyes and let a cold rush of reality flood through her. This bubble had to be popped—mentally, at least.

If there was one certainty in this world, it was that Josh would go. It was who he was. And she needed to keep that sharp little fact in the forefront of her mind.

Josh would go. He would.

Which made him far too dangerous to fall in love with.

CHAPTER EIGHT

THEY found themselves standing in the ticket hall of Holborn station for a third time. Fierce-faced commuters pushed past and flowed round them. Josh looked on as Fern slapped her photocopy of the tube map 'doodle' in frustration.

'We've tried every platform in this station and nowhere does it say where we can get to Aldwych. What are these treasure hunt people playing at?'

He drew her to one side of the ticket hall, out of the way of a woman with a vicious-looking trolley case. 'Are you sure we're in the right place?'

She nodded vigorously. 'It was quite clear on that map at the V&A and, anyway, I remember going there when I was a child to visit Dad at work. For a few years he had an office there. There was a little connecting track, a branch line, that went from Holborn to Aldwych and back again.'

Now she mentioned it, he could remember the

tail-like line on the map in the museum. He turned the map in Fern's hand round to get a better look. There it was again, clear as day.

Another treasure hunt team, the one they least wanted to see—Aidan and Kate—came dashing up the escalator. He and Fern were losing their lead. If they didn't get a move on now they'd be out of the race. He turned on the spot, looking for inspiration, a sign, a map… anything.

A map! He ran over to the poster-sized tube map on the wall. The little dark blue spur and Aldwych station were missing from the Piccadilly line. 'Fern! Over here.' He pressed his finger on to the map. 'It's disappeared.'

She looked at the map, then back at him, clearly worried. 'That's impossible! It can't have just vanished!'

He stared hard at the blank space on the map. 'No,' he said slowly and leaned in close so the other team having a conflab at the top of the escalator couldn't hear, 'but they could have closed it down.' He lifted his eyebrows and waited.

Her eyes widened. 'You're right! I have a vague memory of a news story…oh, years ago.'

He steered her casually to the barrier and they

touched their tickets to the pad so it whooshed open. Once on the other side, he tried to give a good impression of being 'clueless'. The other team were watching them closely and he didn't want to give anything away.

A man in uniform was standing to one side and they approached him. He let Fern talk. She was so sweet and unassuming that people just fell over themselves to help her. Like him, really.

'Excuse me?'

Did he notice a little flutter of the eyelashes there? She was really working it.

'Am I right in thinking Aldwych station is no longer in operation?'

The guard's gruff demeanour melted. 'That's right, love.'

'So we can't get a train there?'

He shook his head. 'Not since 1994, but the station's still there. It gets used for filming and such. Last thing they did there was…oh, what was it called? Some period drama. I'll get it in a—'

'Thank you.' Fern beamed at him. 'Thank you so much.'

They grinned at each other and were about to dash out of the exit when they spotted Kate and Aidan edging their way. Blooming cheek.

'I don't know about you, but I don't really want those two riding our coat tails. We worked this one out and they haven't done anything but stand there and eavesdrop.'

Fern looked across at Kate and narrowed her eyes. 'What do you have in mind?'

'I think we should head down the escalator. They'll think we've got a juicy tip from the guard and follow us, at which point we'll double back, lose them and proceed as planned.'

One side of her mouth worked in a cheeky little smile. 'I like the way you think, Adams.'

'There is way more to like about me than that, Chambers.'

Was he flirting with her? With Fern? He thought he just might be. And, much to his surprise, it seemed to be working. She hadn't scowled or backed away. The fact she was standing there, a mischievous glint in her eye, made his blood heat by a few degrees.

'Let's do it,' he said. Quickly, he added silently. Before the whole flirting-with-Fern thing pushed the plan straight out of his brain.

They walked calmly back through the ticket barriers, trying to look as if they were *trying* to look nonchalant, all the time aware of the other team's piercing looks. Kate wasn't smiling at him now. Good. He didn't want her to.

Then, just as they neared the top of the escalators, prompted by a tiny signal, more a feeling than a gesture, they started to run. When he was halfway down he glanced back and spotted Kate pointing in their direction and muttering angrily to her brother. A split second later they were on the top step of the escalator, running down towards them.

'It's working!'

Fern didn't answer. She was too busy trying to slide past the people queued up on the right side of the escalator. Just near the bottom she stopped, her path blocked by a pair of studenty-looking types and their hefty rucksacks.

'Excuse me!' she said loudly enough to be heard. They turned and stared blankly at her. Obviously from out of town.

The thumping footsteps behind them on the escalator were getting louder. They didn't have time for this.

'Move!' he yelled, jumping past Fern. Now they got the picture. The escalator steps had flattened out and the pair of tourists scurried away, dragging their backpacks after them.

Kate and Aidan were hot on their heels now. He

and Fern made a break to the left, aiming for the Central line. Holborn station was a maze of little tunnels, full of steps, that curved and criss-crossed. It was a blessing in disguise that they'd spent the better part of twenty minutes exploring it earlier, looking for the connection to Aldwych.

They ran on to the Central line platform and immediately dashed out of the exit and circled back to take the main escalators up to ground level. They didn't stop running until they were fifty feet away from the station entrance.

'Can you see them?' Fern could hardly talk. The words were coming out as little breathy squeaks.

He shook his head and swallowed in an effort to moisten his mouth. 'No. I think we lost them.'

She collapsed against the wall of the nearest building, but he tugged her to stand again. 'Come on, it won't take them long to get back on track.'

They jogged down Kingsway and into Aldwych as fast as their pounding hearts and aching lungs would allow them. And there, where Aldwych joined The Strand, they found what they were looking for.

At eye level it was identical to many other abandoned buildings. A grille covered part of the entrance and a chipboard door, secured with a cheap padlock, the other part. If they stepped back and looked above the first storey, its true identity became apparent. Its broad arched façade and its browny-red tiles were identical to many other turn-of-the-century underground stations. And yet hundreds of people probably bustled past this building every day, never appreciating its true beauty. Even mouldering away, not realising its potential and cluttered with the debris of years, it was a stunning piece of architecture.

Fern rattled the grille and peered through into the darkness. 'Perhaps there's another entrance.'

He didn't answer, too caught in a moment of revelation about the woman standing in front of him. He'd been just as blinkered, just as guilty of not appreciating the beauty of the familiar. Because she *was* beautiful, and not just because of her fine bone structure and blonde hair. She was brave. She had an ability to sit tight and stick out situations that he would have run from.

All those years, letting her parents mollycoddle her because she understood how painful it had been for them to lose one child and how scared they were of losing another. It couldn't have been easy. Practically impossible if it'd been him. More than a few days at a time on the same island where Ryan had died made his feet itchy. The thoughts and memories were definitely easier to ignore a few thousand miles away.

Silently he followed Fern round the corner into Surrey Street. He hardly noticed the beaming Secret London marshal who welcomed them and gave them their next clue.

'This is where you'll be staying tonight,' the woman said, 'carrying on the subterranean theme of the day, but first you have a couple more stops to make.'

Inwardly he groaned. The enforced closeness of the underground was starting to suffocate him. He needed air, open spaces. He needed to be able to move, to run. Most of all, he needed to put more than half an inch between himself and Fern before they ended up in a situation one or both of them would regret.

'Find London's original fish market for a true taste of the city.'

Fern inspected every word of the clue with care. They'd made the mistake of glossing over the wording of one yesterday and, if she had one thing going for her, it was that she learned from her mistakes.

'Fish market. That would be Billingsgate. Even I know that,' Josh said, picking up his backpack and getting ready to go.

She held up a hand, palm outwards, to delay him. 'It says *original*. I think they mean the old market building, not the current one. It moved a while back to the Isle of Dogs.'

He leaned in to look over her shoulder and just his breath touching the skin of her neck made her feel hot all over. The fact that the bright summer morning had turned into a muggy, overcast afternoon did not help.

'Is it close?'

No, she answered silently, but you are. Too close. Or maybe just not close enough…

'I'll check the map.' She handed him the clue and got out the guidebook they'd bought yesterday. It had been very helpful in finding local landmarks and attractions as well as roads and stations. 'If we go to Monument, it's only four stops.'

The light went out of his eyes. 'Couldn't we take the bus or walk?'

'We could, but the underground is by far the quickest way.'

He rubbed his face with his hand. 'I'm starting to feel like a rat in a tunnel.'

For the first time since the start of the treasure hunt he seemed tired, and not just physically tired. That worried her. Josh was usually bursting with energy and enthusiasm for everything he did. She looked up at the darkening sky, ugly with yellow-tinged clouds.

'We'll stay dry that way. I think it's going to rain.'

The air was certainly thick with the promise of…something.

The large red bucket on the floor was full of grey slippery things, endlessly twisting and turning. Fern's stomach rolled over. Eels had always looked repulsive to her. She looked back at the old-fashioned East End fish stall parked out the back of Customs House, next to where Old Billingsgate Fish Market used to be.

'What's it going to be, Fern? You choose and I'll pick from what's left. You know me—I'll eat anything.'

At the front of the stall, lined up in squat polystyrene cups, were a choice of winkles, whelks, oysters and jellied eels. Each team member had to eat one cup to fulfil the challenge. *True taste of the city,* indeed! She'd bet the treasure hunt organisers were laughing their socks off about this one. What about pie and mash, or fish and chips?

Absolutely none of the options appealed to her. Maybe the oysters. They were slimy but not nearly as revolting as the dark, muddy-looking winkles. She reached for the cup but, as her fingers made contact with the textured outer surface, she pulled her hand back again and reached for another cup.

Josh gripped her shoulder. 'Jellied eels? Are you sure?'

She nodded, even though the thick grey and white lumps in the bottom of the cup were starting to make her insides swirl.

'Liquor?' the stallholder asked, offering her a jug full of dark green liquid.

'What's in it?' Her voice came out faint and shaky.

Josh put a reassuring hand on her arm. 'The green colour comes from the parsley. It's just like gravy, isn't it?'

The stallholder nodded. 'Although, sometimes the stock is made from—'

Fern held up a warning hand and turned her

head away. 'You know what? I think I'd rather not know.'

Josh reached forward and picked up the cup of oysters. Fern held her cup up so the man could pour some 'liquor' in it. Something warm and wet might make it slide down more quickly. Okay. She picked up a plastic fork. Here goes…

Ten seconds later she was still staring at the contents of the cup, the only sound in her ears the bumping of the live eels as they writhed in the bucket. She was sure the panini from lunch was about to make a return visit.

She closed her eyes. Come on, you can do this! It might not taste nice, but it's not going to kill you. Just remember that.

Keeping her eyes shut, she brought the fork to her mouth and popped the first bit of eel inside, careful to keep it away from her tongue. The plan was to chew it as little as possible and take a swig of the green gravy to wash it down. Despite the urge to propel it out of her mouth with her tongue, she managed it. And then another piece, and another.

Eventually she opened her eyes. One last piece of soggy-looking eel was sitting in the bottom of her cup. Almost there. She threw it into her mouth, but tried to swallow too quickly and it lodged in the back of her throat. She gagged and the whole lot threatened to come back up again.

The urge to be sick bent her forward. One of her hands pressed against her stomach, the other covered her mouth. She got a great view of the red bucket as she leaned over, its contents whipping around in a frenzy.

Oh, Lord…

A warm, strong hand rubbed her back. And she heard his voice, whispering words of encouragement, just as he'd done on top of the crane. The rising tide of nausea swelled, then subsided.

She swallowed hard and the muscles of her oesophagus contracted, pushing the lump of eel down inside her. She stood upright and held on to Josh while she waited for her stomach to stop protesting. It couldn't have churned more if it had been live eels thrashing around inside her.

'Let's get some air.' Josh's arm came round her and he led her to the railing at the river's edge. Now, the Thames wasn't the most fragrant of rivers but, compared to the overpowering wafts from the fish stall, it seemed like fresh mountain air. She sucked it into her lungs in great gasps.

'Better?' There was such a look of tender compassion in his eyes that she was very tempted to cry.

She nodded. 'A little.' Resting her elbows on the thin black railing, she bowed her head.

'You were incredible just then,' he said in a faraway voice.

She shook her head, still looking at her feet. 'I almost threw up. Hardly impressive.'

'Look at me.' He pulled her gently until she was standing, his hands on her shoulders, and he was looking deeply into her eyes. 'Don't sell yourself short, okay? I know how hard that was for you. Believe me, I never thought I'd live to see the day when you ate eel. You're stronger than you realise. In fact, you're stronger than we all realised—especially me.'

She didn't know what to say to that. Everything faded away—the sound of the river lapping against the embankment, the low golden sun on the horizon peeking under the gathering storm clouds and warming the riverside buildings—all of it.

Josh's eyes flicked downwards. He was looking at her mouth, her lips. Her stomach rolled again, but this time it was a pleasant fluttery sensation. She'd been here before. She knew that look on his face. He was going to kiss her and, heaven help her, she desperately wanted him to.

A passing barge hooted its horn and suddenly the rest of the world came rushing back in. Josh stepped away and looked back at the stall. 'I should eat those oysters. Here—' he fetched a bottle of mineral water and thrust it towards her '—you might want this.'

'Thanks,' she mumbled. Josh, about to kiss her? Yeah, right. Not when she probably tasted of eels. She shuddered and gulped down half the bottle of water in one go. Then she rummaged in her backpack for some mints, only really satisfied when the water was gone and the air in her mouth was cold and sharp.

Josh finished his oysters with the minimum of fuss, of course. Fern stood and waited for him as far away from the red bucket and the fish stall as possible. A treasure hunt marshal standing close by offered her the next clue.

'Well done. You're only the second team to have arrived here.'

Fern just nodded and her fingers folded round the envelope. She wanted to kiss Josh. It was all she could think about at the moment. The treasure hunt faded into insignificance.

The only problem was that kissing him would get her nowhere. They'd kissed before and he'd disappeared from her life for almost a year, leaving her aching, yearning for more. It would be the same this time. The pattern would repeat itself.

If she were honest with herself, she'd have to admit that she'd been aching for him quietly, in the background of her life, for the last fifteen years. She didn't want to ache for him any more. It took too much strength, too much energy, to ignore. Yet…she still wanted to kiss him.

A rumble of thunder rolled around in the distance. Fern sucked in a breath and contemplated a new and frightening idea.

Holding back, waiting for Josh, hadn't worked, had it? She might have been able to deaden her feelings for him in the intervening years, shoring herself up with protective barriers, but it had only taken a short time with him for all those dormant feelings to painfully rise to the surface. She hadn't stopped loving him. She'd just numbed herself to a point where she had been able to bury those feelings. Well, no more.

He was joking with the stallholder while he

sipped his bottle of water now, his easy charm winning the old Cockney over instantly. She smiled.

She loved Josh.

There. She'd admitted it to herself. She'd always loved him, ever since she'd been old enough to notice that maybe boys weren't yucky after all. Over the years that love had changed, matured, deepened into an intense ball of feelings that threatened to overwhelm her.

She ought to feel frightened but somehow she wasn't. She was floating, light and free, as the evening sun warmed her face and a gust of breeze lifted the fine hair that had fallen out of her ponytail.

Josh bounded over to her. 'What next?'

Exactly. What next? Where did she go from here?

'Fern? What does the clue say?'

'Oh!' She stared at the envelope gripped lightly between her fingers. 'I don't know. I haven't opened it yet.'

The thunder growled and there was a faint flash of lightning on the other side of the river. Fern was doing her best to follow Josh's long strides up the lane from Billingsgate Market to St Dunstan's Church, their next destination.

The square tower and pointed spire poked above the surrounding buildings. Tucked away in an alleyway, they found the arched doorway which gave them entrance. Fern ran through it and stopped.

'Wow!'

Instead of the musty air and vaulted ceiling of a centuries-old church, it was as if she'd stumbled into a corner of Eden. The ancient stone walls were still in place, with their ornate arched window frames, but where the pews should have been was a garden—stone paths, drooping shrubs and a riot of colour and a softly gurgling fountain. Another world amidst the pollution-stained buildings and grimy streets.

The roof was long gone and the heavy grey clouds overhead made it seem like twilight. The setting sun sent lancing rays to bathe the foliage in orange light.

Josh's hand laced through hers and she felt him tug her forwards. 'Come on,' he said softly. 'We're looking for the east wall. The next clue has to be hidden there somewhere.'

Her feet dragged as he pulled her along. This

place was a real treasure, somewhere she would never have known about if not for Josh and his hare-brained idea to take part in the treasure hunt.

He was slightly in front of her, totally focused on searching the shrubbery for an envelope. There were so many things she wouldn't have experienced if not for this man. She smiled. Salsa dancing in Covent Garden, juggling in a fruit market, the sheer rush of adrenaline and feeling of triumph, knowing they were doing well in the race to the next clue. Still smiling, she winced. Oh, yes, and the revolting eels. But she'd done it; she'd survived.

And he'd brought her much more than that: friendship, faith in her abilities when she had none, love—even though he didn't know it. She wasn't ready to let go of this yet, wasn't ready to let him walk out of her life and disappear again without greedily grabbing for more.

'Here it is!' Josh's shout coincided with a great crack of thunder overhead and the heavens opened. They ran towards a tower, where the branches of the trees had grown through the gaping windows. A large drop of rain splashed on her forehead and the missing roof suddenly became very obvious.

As she stood there, flattened against a wall while Josh snapped a picture of whatever it was they were supposed to take a picture of, she started to wonder whether there was something better than just *aching* for him for another ten years once he disappeared again.

Maybe a little time with him, a little piece of his heart, would be better than nothing. And whatever they might have could build into *something*. It might not, but she'd never know if she never took the chance.

She found a spot under a thick branch thrusting through one of the glassless windows where the rain wasn't falling so hard. She reached out and grabbed a handful of Josh's T-shirt and pulled him close so he was covered too.

Still concentrating on the camera, he shook the water out of his hair. Her pulse began to gallop. He was very sexy when he was damp, and he was only a few inches from her.

He stopped checking the camera and smiled at her. 'Back to Aldwych tube station. Do you want to wait here for a minute or two or shall we just get going?' He stuffed the camera into his pocket, then flinched and let out a yell as a big drop of water hit him on the back of the head and rolled down between his shoulder blades. 'Not much shelter here, is there?'

She looked at him, suddenly feeling very serious. 'It's enough.'

Rain was running down his face and she reached up to smooth it away from his cheeks, to explore the damp spikes of his hair with her fingertips.

Josh froze. The look in her eyes totally floored him—so full of warmth and tenderness and… desire…for him. He shouldn't want her to look at him that way but, oh boy, he did.

Slowly, she raised herself up on to her tiptoes, pulled his head towards her and brought his lips to meet hers. His stomach tightened and his heart pounded. He'd been waiting for this, wanting it, ever since he'd planted that celebratory peck on her lips outside the National Gallery. Maybe longer than that. Maybe his pulse was hammering in his ears because he'd wanted this for years. The strength of his response frightened him.

This was soft, gentle Fern brushing her lips across his, making every cell in his body ache with sweet anticipation. He needed to be gentle too, take it slow…oh, hell.

Her moist tongue traced along his upper lip and

he knew he was on the verge of losing it, of crushing her against the rough stone wall and exploring every inch of her with his hands and mouth. He wound one arm round her, pulling her to him, and curved the other hand behind her head, his fingers stroking the soft skin of her neck. She made the most delightful little sound, part moan, part sigh, then deepened the kiss and pressed herself even closer to him.

All control slid out of his grasp. There was certainly nothing soft or gentle about the way she was kissing him now. It blew his mind.

When they'd kissed before, she'd been timid, innocent. This…this was just…hot. He smiled against her lips and moved to taste the rain-soaked skin of her jaw, her ear lobes, the soft space slightly below that on her neck. She arched against him.

Sweet little Fern was turning him inside out with need. He was both blindsided and completely aroused.

She turned her face towards him, guiding his mouth back towards hers with a firm hand behind his head. He stopped thinking then, let himself go with the flow. He couldn't get enough of her and so he tasted and tasted and tasted…

They broke apart, panting, and she collapsed against his chest. He was literally dragging the breath into his lungs. They were both soaked through, their hair plastered to their heads, beads of rain running off the end of her ponytail.

'Oh.'

That one noise made his need for her grow to shattering proportions.

She closed her eyes. 'I can't breathe.'

He kissed the top of her head and brought his arms around her, trying to keep the rain off, trying to warm her, even though he knew it was a pointless gesture. He laughed, low in the back of his throat. 'I know. Tell me about it! I—'

Suddenly she was pushing against him, staggering backwards and clutching at her throat.

'No…' she heaved in another breath, going pink in the face '…I mean I really…can't… breathe!'

CHAPTER NINE

JOSH punched the coffee machine in the hospital hallway. Not because it was malfunctioning, but because he really needed something to punch.

It had been a relief to get away from Fern's cubicle for a few seconds. It was way too intense in there. At least, that was what he'd thought when he'd pushed the curtain aside. Now he was out here, all he wanted to do was rush back and check she was still okay.

The machine spat out his coffee and he grabbed the cup and sat down on one of the intended-to-be-indestructible upholstered foam chairs nearby and took a scalding mouthful.

He hated hospitals. And, yes, he knew everyone said they hated hospitals, but it was more than the clinical smell that bugged him. It was the endless waiting, the enforced cheerfulness while you visited someone you knew wasn't going to make it.

An image of a pale, bald, skinny Ryan flashed into his head and he bounced it away. That was *not* Ryan. Ryan had been full of life and mischief and fun with his tufty blond hair and his devilish blue eyes. He refused to remember him as anything else.

Josh's shoulders sagged. Ryan had never had the chance to do all the things they'd both planned to do when they grew up. So Josh had done them for him—and more. A life was a terrible thing to waste, so he packed as much in as he could so he would never be guilty of that.

He took one more sip of the coffee, then left the cardboard cup on the low table in the seating area. His brain told him that Fern hadn't had a relapse in the three minutes he'd been away, but he needed hard physical evidence. He needed to see her pale skin regain its colour and the sparkle back in her eyes—so like her brother's.

He took a shaky breath. For a moment there, when the ambulance had screamed up outside, its sirens wailing, he'd had the urge to run. That journey, with Fern gasping for breath, strapped down on to a trolley with one of those plastic masks on her face, had been the single most terrifying experience of his life.

He was such a coward. For a split second he'd been really selfish, had thought of nothing but his need to escape the maelstrom of emotions. He'd even tried to rationalise that she'd be better off if he called her parents and left them all to it. What a wimp! He didn't deserve that adoring look he'd seen in her eyes just before she'd kissed him.

Back in the emergency department, he ducked through the curtain to Fern's cubicle and instantly reached for her hand. A doctor was checking her over, the oxygen mask was off and a hint of pink was returning to her cheeks. When the doctor was finished she slotted the notes back into the space at the end of the trolley.

'Severe allergic reaction,' she said, keeping her eyes firmly on Fern.

Josh's heart began to drum. 'You mean, anaphyalctic shock?'

The doctor shook her head. 'Not quite that drastic, but still pretty nasty—and probably a little bit scary.'

Now he knew why the British were considered masters of understatement. A little bit scary? A little bit? He cleared his throat. 'You know what set it off?'

His gaze shifted to Fern, who was now turning an attractive shade of beetroot.

The doctor clipped a pen back into the pocket of her white coat. 'It seems Miss Chambers is allergic to shellfish.'

'Shellfish? But she didn't have any shellfish. I was the only one who—'

The doctor blinked, then continued. 'Well, thankfully, because of the nature of the…exposure…to the allergen, she only came into contact with a small amount. Just enough to give her a nasty shock by restricting the airways slightly.' She looked firmly at Fern. 'You'll have to be extremely careful in future. I'll make sure a nurse brings you an epi-pen while you wait and shows you how to use it. I'll also be sending a letter to your GP.'

Josh dropped into the hard plastic chair beside the trolley. Oh, Lord, it had been *his* fault, *his* oysters that had caused the whole emergency. And all because he couldn't keep his hands—or, more importantly, his lips—to himself. He couldn't have shown a bit of restraint for a few more days?

This was where 'going with the flow', trusting his instincts, had got him. He'd broken his promise to Ryan and had put Fern in danger. What kind of friend was he? What kind of protector?

Fern sat up on the trolley. 'Can I go soon?'

He whipped his head round to look at her. What she crazy? She needed to stay here where it was safe, where nothing else could happen to her.

The doctor pressed her lips together and thought for a moment. 'I'd like to keep an eye on you for another hour or so, but the drugs the paramedics gave you seem to have had the desired effect, and you don't seem to be having any adverse reactions.'

'You see, we're taking part in a treasure hunt and we need to get back—'

'Fern!' He was standing now, gripping her hand a little harder than necessary to be comforting.

She scowled at him and looked hopefully at the doctor.

'I don't see why not. You've been here a couple of hours already, but I'd like you to wait another hour before I discharge you—and only then if there is someone to keep a constant eye on you for the next twenty-four hours.'

They both looked at him. He nodded.

The doctor looked satisfied, gave a slight nod in return and pulled the curtain open. 'See you in an hour.'

Fern swung herself round so her legs dangled

over the edge of the bed. 'Come here,' she said, opening her arms.

He took a step towards her and wrapped his arms around her, staring over her shoulder as she squeezed him.

'Thank you,' she whispered in his ear. 'Thank you for taking care of me.'

He felt his body go rigid. How could she say that? He'd been a nervous wreck. Hell, he'd very nearly split because he couldn't face seeing her like that, gasping for breath. He'd been so sure she was going to…

He'd been nothing but a coward, for all his talk of being afraid of nothing. He now knew he was terrified of losing Fern. He cared about her too much. He might even… No, that thought was scarier still. He wasn't going there.

She placed her delicate hand softly on his cheek and sat back. 'I can't believe I got to the ripe old age of twenty-eight and never knew I was allergic to shellfish.'

'But you never eat it.'

She smiled at him. 'Yes, but that's because I always thought I was unadventurous, not because I knew it would do me harm.'

He nodded slowly.

'It must be one of those instincts you keep telling me about,' she said brightly. 'Somewhere deep down I knew I should stay away from it.'

He bobbed his head again, but his mind was racing away.

His fault. His oysters. His kiss.

He'd failed. Not only had he not kept her safe, he'd been the one to put her life in danger. And that had been only in a physical sense. Something was building between them and, once again, he'd been too dense and slow to spot it until it was too late. Yet he couldn't let it happen.

If they got together, he knew for a fact that he would end up damaging her emotionally too, and that was something he was not prepared to do. He looked at her as she sank back down against the raised end of the trolley. She was staring at him, a slight frown clouding her lovely features.

That instinct, he whispered silently. *Trust it. Trust that little voice inside your head that's telling you to stay away from me.*

'It's nine-forty! Where is she?' Fern yanked the cubicle curtain open and looked up and down the corridor of the Emergency Department. Only twenty minutes left until they were officially out of the treasure hunt. That doctor needed to discharge her. Now.

Josh was instantly beside her. 'Are you *sure* they didn't give you too big a dose of that adrenaline-type drug?'

She shook her head, still looking up and down the corridor. 'I don't think so. I feel fine.'

He tugged at her arm. 'We don't have to keep going with the treasure hunt, you know. I won't be angry. We tried our best—it just didn't work out, that's all.'

'I am *not* giving up.'

She'd never felt so certain about anything in her whole life. This was a pivotal moment, she was sure of it. No way could she just sink back into the soggy greyness of her everyday life without knowing she had given whatever this was that was happening with Josh every last shot.

Every minute left racing for the prize money meant another minute with him, and those seconds were too precious to waste. What had that kiss meant to him? How did he really feel about her? She needed to find out the answers to these questions or it would haunt her for the rest of her life.

A hand appeared on the edge of the curtain and pulled it open. They both jumped.

'Hello, love. I thought I'd drop by and see how you were doing before I get another shout. How're you doing?'

Fern grinned at the big bear of a man in a green paramedic's uniform standing just outside the cubicle. 'Hi, Bruce. I'm fine now. Just waiting to be discharged. Thank you so much for coming to my rescue.'

'Any time.'

Then, just because she couldn't help it, she looked at her watch. Seventeen minutes. Her stomach dropped.

A nurse suddenly appeared beside Bruce. 'Fern Chambers? I just need you to sign these.'

The paperwork seemed to take for ever, but in reality it probably only took a minute. She thrust the clipboard and pen back at the nurse. Bruce, who had been discussing something in low tones with a worried-looking Josh, clapped her on the shoulder.

'Well, if that's you done, I'll be off. Just glad I could help.' He turned to Josh. 'Now, you just look after her, mate.'

Josh looked unusually grim. 'That's the plan.'

Bruce nodded and disappeared back towards the ambulance bay. Fern's stomach fluttered.

Twelve minutes left! How on earth were she and Josh going to make it back to Aldwych Station in that amount of time? They'd need a miracle, or at the very least a police escort!

She pushed past Josh. 'Bruce!'

The burly paramedic, just about to push the swing doors at the end of the corridor, stopped and turned. She ran up to him, leaving Josh to deal with her backpack.

'You know when you said, "Any time"? Did you really mean it?'

Josh gripped on to the chair in the back of the ambulance as it hurtled round a corner, its blue lights flashing and its sirens wailing.

'I'm going to be in so much…*trouble*…if anyone finds out about this,' Bruce yelled from the front of the ambulance as his partner yanked the steering wheel in the opposite direction. 'Just as long as you two know that, if we get a shout, you will have to use your feet instead!'

Fern, who was sitting on the edge of the trolley, her knuckles going white with the effort of hanging on, leaned forward and shouted back to him. 'We really appreciate this, Bruce. Don't we, Josh?'

His voice felt thick and scratchy and it was an

effort to make sure he was heard above the wail of the sirens. 'Yeah.'

'You're a real sweetie!' Fern added and Bruce blushed.

The ambulance turned again and Josh was almost jolted off his seat. He frowned. He'd always thought he'd enjoy a ride in an ambulance or police car, foot to the floor, sirens screaming, but, to be honest, he was still reeling from the first ride of the day—and from all that had happened immediately before it.

Today, instead of enjoying the buzz of the adrenaline rush, he'd felt lost and out of control—not a pleasant experience.

Life was so fragile. *People* were so fragile. Yet he'd bulldozed his way through life with very little respect for that fact. Fern was worth more than his careless regard. A cold knife sliced through him as he realised how much he'd taken her for granted, had always expected her to be there. Today's scare had shown him just how easy it would be for her to…

The urge to scoop her up and kiss her senseless, even in the midst of the speeding, clattering ambulance, almost overwhelmed him. However, he was starting to realise that some instincts were meant to be resisted. Yes, if he and Fern got together it would be wonderful for a while, but it would ultimately end in disaster. Much safer for him to be on one continent and her to be on another.

The ambulance braked sharply and Fern catapulted off the trolley and landed on top of him. She giggled while he checked her for bruises, then pulled herself to stand.

'Two minutes to spare. Bruce, you are truly a star!' She blew him a kiss. 'And I meant what I said about the prize money. If we win, the ambulance station charity box gets five hundred pounds.'

They clambered out the back of the ambulance and ran into the abandoned station. The treasure hunt marshal standing by the door made another tick on his clipboard. He looked up at them.

'The bad news is you're the twenty-sixth couple to arrive tonight.'

Fern looked as if someone had asked her to eat eels again.

'But the good news is that seven of those teams have been disqualified for either visiting the wrong tube stations this afternoon, missing some out altogether or not having the required photographs in the right order. Congratulations! You're still in the running.'

Fern squealed and jumped up and down. Josh tried to look suitably triumphant, but inside he was wondering how he could stand another day and a half with Fern when he knew he was going to have to say goodbye to her again so soon.

The thought of leaving her tore at him, but at least then they might be able to return to how they'd been. They'd pick up their friendship again and she'd be happy and safe. Much more terrifying was the thought of taking the unmarked road ahead, of loving her…and losing her.

If she could sleep here, thought Fern, she'd probably be able to sleep anywhere. The remaining forty competitors were camped down on one of the disused platforms of Aldwych underground station. The teams, now deep in competitive mode, were keeping themselves to themselves and pairs of sleeping bags and foam mattresses were dotted along the vast flat concrete strip.

During the day, tube stations were normally stifling with the heat of too many bodies crammed into too little space. Even the gusts of air that blew down the platform heralding the arrival of a train were warm—a stale version of a tropical breeze. But, at ten past midnight, in a station that hadn't seen traffic in more than a decade, it was decidedly chilly.

She wanted so badly for Josh to shuffle up against her again as he had done in the caves, but he was turned away from her, a good foot between them, even though their mattresses were butted up against each other.

Taking a deep breath, she rolled over to face him. He was so still. Too still. He wasn't asleep.

She slid her legs towards him and moved her body closer, the slippery outer cover of the sleeping bag smoothing her way. Slowly, she slid an arm around him and pressed her face up against his solid back. A few seconds later she moved her arm again. It was difficult to find a comfortable place to rest it.

Still Josh didn't move. She closed her eyes, partly out of embarrassment. Why didn't he touch her back? A few hours ago things had been very different indeed. What was it about her? Every time she kissed this man, he ran a thousand miles.

She had a choice now. She could remove her

arm and retreat to the cold edge of her mattress or she could stay where she was.

There really was no comfortable way to lie up against six foot of solid male who obviously didn't want to be cuddled. Still, she wasn't giving up. Consciously, she relaxed her muscles and, before she settled into stillness, she kissed the broad warmth of his back through his T-shirt.

He stopped breathing. Unable to do anything else, she held her own breath too while the wind whistled distantly in the abandoned tunnel. Then, all in one move, Josh turned towards her, collected her up in his arms and rolled her with him so they ended up facing the other direction, his large frame wrapped around her, cradling her.

She stroked the arm that was clamped possessively across her front. *This* was where she'd wanted to be. Oh, yes, she thought as he nuzzled against her neck, his breath warming her cheek, this was definitely what she'd had in mind.

Today, he'd been fantastic. He'd called the ambulance, done all the right things, hardly left her side. For once she'd been able to rely on him. In the dark she frowned. No, Josh wasn't unreliable. It was just that his wandering nature meant that he couldn't be counted on to be there when it mattered. But tonight she'd needed him—it had mattered, big time—and he'd been there.

It couldn't have been easy for him to watch her like that. If the tables had been turned, she'd have been a mess. At the time, she'd been too busy just finding the next breath to be scared, but Josh… He'd had to watch, helpless, as the paramedics had arrived and administered the intramuscular injection that had flooded her system with chemicals that allowed her narrowed airways to expand.

That must have killed him—Josh, with his dynamic, take charge, go-get-'em personality.

She sighed. He lived life *right*.

Now she understood why, after Ryan's death, he'd been driven to move, live, explore. She'd let her parents teach her how to hibernate instead, always protected from the world by good common sense, relevant safety information and a whopping dollop of fear. Well, it was time for the tide to turn, for her to live, not to hide, as Josh had put it.

His hand reached over her face and brushed away a section of hair that had fallen across her cheek. She lay there, giving in to the dizzying feeling of his touch as he stroked her hair, lulling her into a hypnotic state.

It was more than just chemistry between her and Josh. With every touch, he seemed to be speaking a promise. And, for the first time in years, when a tiny candle of hope flickered into life inside her, she let it burn instead of snuffing it out.

'I can't hear you!' Fern was now whispering so loud people walking past were turning to stop and stare. Josh, who was some distance away on the other side of the dome of St Paul's Cathedral, did some kind of sign language. None of it made any sense.

They were getting nowhere, and that was not good news. As the last team to arrive at the checkpoint last night, they had some catching up to do. She pointed exaggeratedly at a spot halfway between where she was standing and where he was standing. He shrugged.

She started jogging and kept pointing. Finally he got it and started to move towards a place where they could meet up and talk.

'I thought this was supposed to be some kind of clever *whispering* gallery!' he said. 'I'm practically shouting and you're still not hearing anything.'

She shook her head slightly, biting her lip. 'It *should* work. Let's read the instructions through one more time and have another go.'

He nodded and looked over her shoulder as she held the clue up. There were clear directions for the task. The gallery at the base of the dome of St Paul's had an unexpected architectural quirk. How someone had discovered it was anyone's guess. Supposedly, if two people stood diametrically opposite from each other and one whispered against the wall, the acoustics were such that the other person should hear it—only it didn't seem to be happening for her and Josh.

The challenge was simple. One treasure hunt marshal would hand one team member a card which they then read a phrase from. The other team member was supposed to repeat the phrase to a second marshal. When the received whisper matched the phrase printed on the card they could move on.

Josh looked back to where he'd been standing. 'Why don't we swap places?'

'Okay.' It couldn't hurt.

When she reached the marshal, he made a great show of giving her a different card to read. She watched Josh get ready, placing his ear close to the wall, entirely focused as usual. It was less than twenty-four hours to the end of the race now and all the teams were feeling the pressure. At least, that was her guess at Josh's quiet mood. He really wanted to win those vouchers for his parents and had hinted that he needed to concentrate on that for the moment.

That was so like Josh. Thinking of other people first. And, knowing how much his mum and dad needed the break, she was prepared to wait a little longer to discuss the current state of their relationship. She'd waited twelve years to have this opportunity. A few more hours couldn't hurt.

She paused. There was an odd sense of intimacy about this moment. They were at least fifty feet away from each other. Tourists wandered round the gallery, chatting, while they looked down at the chequered stone floor below and then up into the ornate dome. It was busy, full of people, and yet she and Josh were connected. If he spoke, it would seem as if he were standing right beside her.

She looked at the words printed on the card. What would happen if she tucked it away and said what she really wanted to say?

I love you. I'll always love you.

Would she see his eyes widen, his trademark sexy smile slowly curve his lips? And, more importantly, what would he say back?

The words were on the tip of her tongue, ready to be carried to him on a breath. Her pulse quickened and she folded the card in her hand until she could no longer see the random fact about the cathedral.

At sixteen she'd never really had the courage to tell him the strength of her feelings, had merely accepted his judgement that it wouldn't work because he was going away to university. She should have fought harder, spoken up.

But the girl she'd been back then had been incapable of that. Was the woman she was now any more equipped?

Breath filled her lungs and a velvety whisper emerged. 'At three hundred and sixty feet high, the dome of St Paul's is the second largest in the world.'

Coward.

It was five o'clock in the afternoon and Josh was a bundle of nerves. He blew on the dice in his hands and said a silent prayer for sixes. 'Come on,' he whispered as he hurled them across the green felt.

'Oh! Too bad.' Fern's gentle hand made contact with his arm and he jumped. She'd been doing this all day, finding reasons to touch him. It was not helping his resolve to keep his distance. He scooped up the dice, showing a two and a five, and rattled them in his hand.

He'd never been one for regrets, but *if onlys* were haunting him now. *If only* getting together with Fern weren't such a disastrous idea...*if only* he could manage not to break her heart. He sighed.

'Never mind,' she said brightly beside him. 'We'll just keep going.'

She reached out to take the dice from his palm. He was lost in thought and giving her no help; the dice just lay in his half-curled hand. Her fingers tickled his sensitive flesh and the backs of his ears burned. She felt it too, he knew. That slight intake of breath, the subtle flush of colour spreading under her collar-bone.

If only he could forget this stupid challenge, drag Fern away somewhere private and see if he could make that blush spread to her toes. The memory of her kisses the day before flooded through him. It was just as well he wasn't holding the dice any more because they would have been dust in his hand.

Funnily enough, he'd never once thought, *If only we hadn't kissed,* in the last twenty-four hours.

'Your turn again, Josh.' Her hand raised and there was a slight hesitation before she placed a silent palm on his back. Once again she'd made contact. It was as if she was waiting for a signal, a sign that he couldn't give back.

Luckily, the dice were still on the table and he broke contact by leaning forward to pick them up. He was pretty pig-headed and he'd told himself he could handle this. He could smile and be pleasant and, ever so slowly, he would back off and let her down gently. But these little touches of hers brought tiny sparks of sensation that set his defences smouldering.

He felt the two small cubes in his hand and looked around the ornate room, trying to absorb some of the luck that must have flowed here over the centuries. Black's Gentlemen's Club was legendary. Tucked away in the heart of St James's, no one walking past the door would have guessed that the respectable-looking stone building had been one of the most outrageous gambling dens of Regency times.

Fortunes had been made and lost in this very room. And now it was time to make his. All he needed was another double six.

His thoughts were interrupted by a scream of joy from another team a few feet away. The two girls squealed and hugged each other, then collected their next clue from a treasure hunt marshal and left.

So simple and yet so difficult. All his team had to do in this challenge was throw three double sixes to receive the next red envelope. No complicated games of dice or cards. He and Fern had started off well, rolling the first two pairs within a minute of starting, but for the last long ten minutes all they'd come up with were mismatched numbers.

Fern's heart jumped as the dice rumbled across the table. One came to rest with a single spot on top. The other bounced off the padded rim of the table, then rolled to land next to it. A four. She let out a nervous breath.

The location must be getting to her, because she had her own secret bet going. Madness itself. If he threw double ones, she would tell him. Today. It had seemed such a good idea when it had first come to her, but now she was actually scared of the dice rolling that way. She needed more time.

He looked so determined. His head was totally on the race today. More than once, when she'd wanted to bring up the matter of yesterday's kiss, he'd returned to mumbling about his parents and had hurried her along to the next destination. She could wait. At some point today there'd be a lull and she'd have a chance to test the waters.

'Yes!' Josh punched the air with his fist. She'd been too busy day-dreaming to notice the two sixes face upwards on the now still dice. All day she'd been screwing up the courage to touch him, sending him silent messages, but this time thinking didn't even come into it as exuberance replaced frustration.

He seemed to have surprised himself out of his far-away mood too, because he wrapped his arms around her and twirled her around on the spot. When her feet touched the floor again they broke apart, grinning, laughing.

Their eyes connected and she saw something true and deep reflected in the widening pupils. She loved this man. A cloud passed over his expression and she couldn't name the emotion responsible. Doubt? Regret? It melted away as he lowered his head and kissed her.

Their last kiss had been good—passionate, unrestrained—but this one was far sweeter. He kissed her softly, slowly, as if he were trying to tell her something and she sensed an answering ache in him, one identical to the dull throbbing pain she'd carried around inside for so many years that she couldn't remember what it was like to live without it.

She poured all the love and adoration she had for him into the kiss. Could he? Did he feel the same way? Had he been running from his feelings for too long as well?

A gentle cough somewhere else in the room made them freeze. They disentangled themselves and turned to face a treasure hunt marshal holding a red envelope out to them, one eyebrow raised.

'Thanks,' Fern said shakily as she smoothed down her T-shirt and took the clue from the girl. Josh coughed and picked up the dice from the table and offered them to the marshal. He looked so totally adorable, all crumpled and at sixes and sevens.

'Do you want these back?'

The girl shook her head. 'No, it's okay. You can leave them on the table ready for the next team.'

He leaned over and dropped the dice on to the green table top. It was only when Fern stood again, after heaving up her backpack from the floor, that she saw them and almost keeled over.

A little dot was winking cheekily at her from the top of each cube.

CHAPTER TEN

FOR a London summer it was a mild night, but Fern was shivering in his arms. He'd managed to keep his hands off her all evening—which was practically a heroic feat—but this was allowed. This was different. She needed him to keep her safe and warm.

The last night of the treasure hunt was definitely going to be the hardest. No sleeping bags tonight, only rough blankets.

'Are you warm enough, Fern?'

'Yes.' Her teeth chattered as she spoke.

'Are you sure?'

She let out an irritated little noise and burrowed further against him. 'Yes.' The noise was muffled against his jacket.

'Miss Fern Chambers, are you fibbing again?'

A relieved breath whooshed out of her. 'Yes.'

He chuckled and pulled the grey woollen blanket further over them. Tonight they were experiencing a London that most people never saw, mostly because they blinded themselves to it. Tonight they were living like the city's homeless, hunched on a bench in Victoria Embankment Gardens. The Savoy hotel, resplendent in its art deco glamour, was only a stone's throw away, giving the scene a weird sense of contradiction.

Of course, the Secret London teams weren't the only ones huddling on the benches. He wasn't sure their presence was welcomed by the handful of regulars. Even when he'd walked round the park earlier and dished out some of their hard-earned salsa and fruit market cash, some had eyed him suspiciously, although they'd still taken the money. A couple had smiled and thanked him.

He was glad he was here to protect Fern. All his latent caveman tendencies had woken up growling, ready to defend her from any danger. And that was good, because he needed to remember his promise. It was all about keeping Fern safe. How ironic then that he was one of the biggest threats to her happiness at the moment.

She was such a strong woman underneath that fragile exterior. As he stared into the darkness and remembered their adventures over the last few days, he couldn't help but feel warmth spreading in his chest. He was so proud of her.

She'd been terrified at times, but she hadn't let it stop her. The young, sweet girl he remembered had flowered into a feisty, clever, warm and resourceful woman and he'd bet more than five thousand pounds that she had no idea how wonderful she really was.

He couldn't take that generous heart and crush it. He wouldn't.

None of his relationships had survived more than a year—mostly because he was always away. Things tended to start off well but just petered out. No messy emotions. No ugly scenes. And, to be honest, up until now that had never really bothered him.

He just didn't have it in him to stay put in one place and commit. And that was why, when every instinct in his mind and body was screaming for him to make a go of it with Fern, he had to back off. She deserved more than six good months, another four of awkward e-mails and then intermittent texts and calls that would cease before a year was up.

Fern deserved more. Fern deserved forever.

Unfortunately, he was just not the guy to give it to her.

* * *

Josh's fleece was soft against her cheek and she could hear his heart beating. A piece of newspaper, yanked this way and that by the wind, rose into the air as it blew past them, then was snatched down the path by another gust.

He shifted beneath her and she guessed he was reaching for his backpack.

'Would it be okay if I had that last chocolate bar?' he asked.

Fern pressed her lips together. Just the thought of chocolate was making her mouth fill with saliva, but for another hour or two there was only one answer she could give him.

'Yes.'

Funny, at the start of the week she'd found herself in all sorts of difficult situations, grinding that word out between her teeth, wishing she could answer the opposite, but in the last few days she'd hardly noticed it. *Yes* now just slid from her lips. So, much as she hated to admit it, perhaps Lisette had been right. Perhaps she had needed shaking up.

She heard foil rip and—oh, goodness—she could *smell* the chocolate. Her mouth watered so hard she had to lick her lips and swallow.

'Okay,' Josh said with a mouthful of chocolate,

'I'm not convinced you don't want any of this. Do you want half?'

She grinned. 'Oh, go on, then. Yes.'

Her whole life this week had been governed by how people phrased their questions. If Josh had said, Are you sure you don't want to go on this treasure hunt? instead of asking her, 'What do you say?' she'd have been tucked up in her nice warm bed, looking forward to the prospect of one of Lisette's full English breakfasts in a few hours. Somehow she couldn't summon up the energy to be disappointed about that.

She took the slab of crumbly, slightly melted chocolate from him. It was heaven. She savoured every last molecule, even licking her fingers. Josh's breathing went all funny. She sat up to look at him.

'Are you okay?'

'Yes…no…probably.'

She laughed.

'What's so funny?'

She shook her head, tickled by the fact that she wasn't the only one having problems with answers tonight, but unable to tell him why. He looked so gorgeous with his hair sticking up and a boyish frown wrinkling his features that she just had to kiss him. As she moved closer, her eyelids closed. The soft flesh of her lips met his—and then they were gone again.

He shuffled backwards into the corner of the bench.

'Josh? What's wrong?'

He stared back at her with a strange look on his face. 'It's just…I don't think we should do this.'

Sixteen-year-old Fern would have said 'oh' and backed off. Twenty-eight-year-old Fern needed answers more badly than she needed her dignity. 'Why?'

Josh pushed himself to his feet and brushed the blanket away. The evening air was cold on her legs, but it was nothing compared to the icy feeling that ran right through her as he took a few long strides to stand on the path and stare at the traffic rushing along Victoria Embankment and then at the river beyond. A crowd of people in formal dress ambled past, giving them a few curious looks—and a wide berth. She scrambled to stand and join him.

'Why, Josh?'

She knew he was going to move again even before the words had left her mouth and she laid a restraining hand on his arm. He avoided strong emotions, sticky situations. Even a hint of an argument had sent him scurrying for the top of the old apple tree when he was a boy.

He'd probably rather be in a snake-infested pit than having this conversation right now. The gathering hurt in his eyes as he looked at her made her heart cramp. She knew what he had to say wasn't going to be pretty—he'd have kissed her back otherwise—and it was going to kill him to hurt her, but they couldn't leave things hanging for another twelve years. They both needed to work out what was going on between them so they could either act on it or put it behind them.

'I care a great deal about you, Fern.'

Oh, brother! She'd heard this speech in various guises before, from various men. Pretty soon he'd be saying, It's not you; it's me…

He stuck his hands in his pockets. 'I'm not a settle-down-and-get-serious kind of guy; you know that.'

Tears prickled the backs of her eyes. She did know that. Only, deep down, she'd been hoping that was because he hadn't found the right woman. He hadn't found *her*.

'It wouldn't last, Fern. And, if we split up, it's

going to be awkward for everyone, not just us, our parents too. I wouldn't want to be the cause of a rift between them. They've been friends for almost forty years. And then there's…'

He walked away a few steps, then turned and came back again.

'Go on. Say it.'

'There's Ryan.'

Suddenly, the successful, dynamic thirty-two-year-old in front of her reminded her of the ten-year-old Josh, desolate about the death of his pet goldfish, but the moment of vulnerability hardened into something more gruff and familiar.

Oh, she was angry with him for messing her around, for making her fall for him twice as hard, but the knowledge that he still missed Ryan as much as she did poured a big old bucket of water on her smouldering anger.

He scuffed the toe of his trainer on a paving slab. 'I don't want to ruin our friendship.'

Fern put her hands on her hips. The clichés just kept on coming. It was as if he was reeling off a list of excuses, finding reasons not to be with her. She breathed in and held it. That was exactly what this was. Why? Why did he feel the need? She was stumped and, because she had more pressing things on her mind, she pushed it to one side.

'You mentioned Ryan…'

Heaven knew she'd loved her big brother to bits, but he'd had a habit of fouling up her life. Even now, it seemed.

'I promised him—not out loud, but in here—' he thumped his chest with his palm, his voice strained, and a lump closed her throat '—that I would do his job, be his stand-in. And I wouldn't be much of a brother to you if I stood by and let somebody hurt you. Especially if that somebody was me.'

Tears flowed over her lashes. The stupid, noble, wonderful man! She itched to touch him, to smooth the lines in his forehead away with kisses. Josh crossed his arms and looked at her fiercely. Now was not the time to make lip contact.

'You understand, don't you?' he said.

She nodded. Yes, yes, she did. It only made her love him more, but it didn't mean she agreed with his judgement. Knowing Josh, he wasn't going to be swayed easily. A tiny glimmer of hope remained, but it was on the verge of flickering out.

He walked back to the bench and slid into a corner, as if he was barricading himself in. It couldn't have been clearer if he'd used barbed wire and a 'keep out' sign.

Fern sighed and sank into the opposite corner, pulling the edge of the scratchy blanket over her legs. A loud sniff escaped before she could hold it back. She dragged the back of her hand across her eyes.

'Please don't cry.' His voice was thready and hoarse. She looked at him, tears threatening to flood again, and held them back by sheer willpower.

'I don't want to lose you,' he said, staring at the twinkling lights skipping on the river.

She couldn't say anything without opening the floodgates, so she just concentrated on breathing. This was as raw and open and real as she'd seen the ever-cool Josh.

'Let's just agree to forget this and let things go back to the way they were. Okay?'

He waited for her to answer.

She looked at her watch. Two minutes past eleven. Oh, how she wanted to yell *no* at him, tell him to stop giving her excuses, tell him to stop expecting the worst, but she couldn't do it. With one hour to go, she couldn't deprive the Leukaemia Research Trust of vital funds, not when she'd come this close. Damn her conscience! Why couldn't it take a hike?

'Fern?'

'Okay. Yes.' For now.

In exactly fifty eight minutes, she would be starting a conversation with the words, Actually, *no…*

Fern propped her chin on her bent knees and sighed. Josh was a few feet away, tucked into his corner of the bench, his breathing soft and even.

She wanted to kill him.

How, with all that had been swirling in the air between them, had he managed to fall asleep? Maybe it was because he was used to bedding down in unusual places—up trees, hanging off ledges. Whatever the reason, he was out like a light.

Her bottom was going numb and she shifted on the flaky wood. As midnight had approached, she'd been too absorbed in the hands of her watch to notice that Josh had started to doze. If she'd realised, she could have kept him awake by striking up a conversation—about what, she didn't know. Anything to keep him lucid until she could talk to him with complete freedom.

He made a soft grunt and his head lolled further

on to his chest. There was no point in waking him. She knew from experience that a sleepy Josh was grumpy and stubborn, hardly the best frame of mind for the conversation she'd planned.

Would she really have had the nerve to let it all out, tell him how she felt? She wouldn't have chickened out? Even if she knew in her heart he wasn't going to say yes to her? She nodded to herself. Yes, she would have. Even after all that had been said this evening. Crazy, huh? It was just something she had to do, some instinct she needed to follow.

She pulled the blanket up to her chin and huddled further into herself. Josh might be able to kip anywhere, but she'd be surprised beyond belief if she nodded off at all tonight. She was cold, uncomfortable and just the circular thoughts bombing round the racetrack of her brain alone were enough to prevent her from sleeping.

No, she was just going to have to sit it out and wait.

Her eyes were gritty and sore. She probably looked a complete mess. Know what? She didn't care. All she wanted at this precise moment was for coins to hit the bottom of the plastic collection tin she had in her hand and then she could be on her way.

All the teams had been walked up from the park to Charing Cross station and were now rattling collection boxes for London City Radio's homeless charity. The team that collected the most money in one hour would be given the next clue first. The team in second place would get their clue three minutes later, and so on.

If she and Josh were going to win this money, they needed to be somewhere near the top of the list. The final round teams were all fired up and hungry for the prize. Any slip-ups could be fatal.

She checked her watch. Only twenty more minutes before the time was up. Oh, how she hated this. Early-morning commuters bustled past, not even seeing her. They didn't even look at her. On a much smaller level, she knew what it was like to live with a label the world slapped on you whether you liked it or not.

Poor Little Fern… Sensible Old Fern…

The one person she'd always longed to see past the labels was standing right next to her, eyes open, shutters down. But it turned out that, in the end, even he had fallen into the trap.

We can't hurt Poor Little Fern, can we? We

have to keep her safe, smother her in cotton wool. The thought made her want to scream out loud. She'd played the part for too long. At first, it had been to keep her parents happy, to help them realise that they wouldn't lose their only remaining child as well. But, somewhere along the line, the act had become a habit. She'd slipped into living that way. It was comfortable, easy. Boring.

It had taken this week to make her realise that this was not who she was; it was not what she wanted. She glanced across at Josh. Whether she could have what she really wanted was another matter.

The stony silence between them finally got to her. 'What you said last night, about hurting our parents, about Ryan… they're just excuses.'

He turned sharply towards her. 'What the hell are you talking about?'

'Why do you always run, Josh?'

He stared blankly across the station concourse. 'I'm not running. I'm freezing my…rear end off shaking a plastic box in Charing Cross station.'

The look she gave him reflected just how weary she was. 'You know what I mean.'

He didn't answer, just shook his head.

Perhaps he *didn't* know. Perhaps he didn't realise that every time anyone tried to get close, he took off—literally, sometimes. Travelling round the world at the speed of light tended to help in that respect. But, one day, it would all overtake him. Didn't he realise that?

'One day, you'll have to let someone close.'

He made an angry grunt. 'I let people close.'

'Such as?'

'My parents…'

There was an awkward pause. She filled it. 'Whom you see once every couple of months.'

He looked at her crossly. 'I e-mail.' The words were tinged with both guilt and defiance.

She laughed. Had to. 'Very intimate.'

Now he was angry. She could feel it coming at her in waves. This was *so* not how she'd planned this conversation, but she'd been so blooming frustrated with him that she hadn't been able to resist poking the growling monster with a sharp stick.

He let it all out in a rush. 'Look, just because I don't want to start something with you doesn't mean I'm emotionally stunted, okay? There's just not enough mileage in it to warrant us both getting hurt.'

Ouch.

He grunted again. 'I'm fine. I'm as warm and fuzzy and sensitive as the next guy. I even thought about asking Vanessa to marry me. Did Mum ever tell you that?'

She shook her head, speechless.

'Well, maybe I'm not as much of a wreck as you'd like to think. Maybe it's just that I don't feel that way about you. Have you ever considered that?'

He finished abruptly and scared away a commuter who was about to put coins in his tin by scowling at him. It was eight hours past midnight and, even though there were a million words she could now choose from, only one answer represented the truth.

'Yes.'

Of course she'd considered that, feared that. And now he was confirming it in no uncertain terms. However, she'd asked for it, had pushed him for a *real*, honest, true response. It was her own fault if she didn't like what she heard.

Maybe it was the lack of sleep, the bone-deep exhaustion of racing round London for days on end, or the sheer knowledge that her teenage dreams were over, just as surely as if they'd been floating down one of the city's filthy gutters and swirling into the sewers, but she began to cry.

Silent tears streamed down her face as she stared

at the blurry shapes in front of her—passing shadows of people and the departure board.

'Oh, don't do that, love!'

The voice wasn't Josh's. She blinked and a short man in a train driver's uniform came into focus.

'Here—' He thrust a ten pound note at her. He gave Josh a withering look. 'You should be taking care of her, mate, not making her do this.' He shook his head and moved on. Josh swore under his breath.

'Th-thank you,' she stammered, even though the man was well out of earshot. And then she cried harder. Pathetic. It didn't matter what she wanted to be, how she wanted to be thought of. All anyone ever saw was Poor Fragile Little Fern. It was never going to change.

Josh was sure black thunderclouds were gathering over his head. He hadn't been in a mood this bad since…since…

This was why he didn't do complicated, messy, up-close relationships. Something always went wrong. Somebody always got hurt. Somebody always left. He was livid with Fern for poking him in all the sore places of his soul—places he didn't really want to acknowledge existed. She'd made him do stupid things, say stupid things.

Why had he brought Vanessa up? She'd been his last serious—if that was a word that could ever be applied to his relationships—girlfriend. Yes, he'd thought about popping the question, but not in the way he'd let Fern believe. He'd been in a panic because all his friends seemed to be getting married and having babies. The idea had lived all of ten seconds.

He'd seen the look on Fern's face and felt like an utter amoeba. But she'd kept pushing, wouldn't accept his reasons for keeping his distance. How else was he going to keep her at bay? It was her fault, really.

The remaining teams had finished the 'collecting for charity' challenge and were now assembled back in the park. An 'on-the-spot' reporter from the radio station was doing interviews for the breakfast show, talking to the teams as the organisers provided breakfast and tallied up the money from the challenge.

Listening, he started to realise that the radio station had been broadcasting features about the treasure hunt all along, keeping the listening public up-to-date with where the teams were and who was in the lead. He and Fern had been completely unaware of it, too focused on competing to think about the publicity angle.

They'd better not come near him with that microphone. The mood he was in, he was likely to bite the top off.

He looked at Fern, standing beside him, swaying slightly. They'd better not try and interview her, either. She was practically asleep on her feet. Her eyes were pink and puffy and her hair was falling out of her ponytail. On any other day he'd have put his arm round her and given her a hug, then found her somewhere to sit, but not today. It was too dangerous.

First place went to Kate and Aidan. Kate had slashed and knotted her T-shirt in strategic places and it didn't take much to guess why they'd collected so much money. Amazingly, he and Fern came in second. After Fern had started crying—he ignored the twisting in his gut as he thought about that—the money had just flowed in.

A rumble travelled round his hollow stomach, making her eyes widen. She yawned. 'Me too. I hope they're going to feed us soon.'

Continuing the theme, they were going to be consuming leftover food donated by a local sandwich chain, something the branches did regularly for the city's homeless. He couldn't keep his eyes off the two large cardboard boxes guarded by two treasure hunt marshals.

Just about the time he thought he was going to be eaten alive by his own stomach acid, they opened the flaps and pulled out trays of assorted sandwiches, baguettes and wraps. They were a day past their sell-by date, but nobody cared. He made a beeline for the trays, finding them grouped together by type—vegetarian, chicken, seafood—he nabbed the biggest baguette he could find and just dropped on to the grass to eat it.

Fern was some distance away, staring absently into space. For the last three days they'd been glued to each other's sides, eating, sleeping and racing together. It wasn't the same any more. They were pulling apart, thinking independently of each other again. The thought made him feel hollow, but it had to be that way.

'Want one of these?' A marshal offered him an avocado and crayfish sandwich from the seafood tray he was carrying.

'If they're going spare. I think some of the

people over there haven't had any yet.' The guy nodded and moved off.

This was better. Keeping his mind on simple things—food, sleep, travel—was much more comfortable.

Josh hoped the guy came back. He was almost all the way through the baguette and he was still hungry. The crayfish and avocado had looked delicious. And he didn't have to worry about the shellfish content any more.

Disappointment flooded through him and he quickly dammed it. He would not be kissing Fern again any time soon. Maybe in five years' time, when they saw each other at her parents' Christmas do. She'd probably be married by then, with a smart, sensible-looking husband and her toddler on her hip. He stared at the ground. No point getting all upset about it. That was the way it had to be.

The treasure hunt marshal walked back past him. 'Hey! Any of those sandwiches left?'

The guy shook his head. 'Nope, sorry. Just gave the last one to the blonde over there. She seemed a bit spaced out. Took one, though.'

Josh nodded. And then he went very still.

Crayfish.

He hoped Fern had paid attention to what she was putting in her mouth, but she said she hadn't had a wink last night and she was so sleep-deprived she might not have…

His head jerked round just in time to see Fern collapse on to the ground, an open sandwich carton in her hand.

Fern hit the grass with a thud. 'Ouch!' Stupid, stupid trainers. Stupid, stupid lumps in the deceptively flat-looking grass. Her dignity was wounded enough already. She didn't need total humiliation.

She stared at the sandwich in her hand. She'd decided to discard the soggy bits of lettuce and wondered if she'd be able to fling them in the bin from here. She really didn't have the energy to get up at the moment.

But, before she could say *lollo rosso*, a huge pair of arms scooped her up and crushed her to a warm, solid chest. She recognised that familiar masculine scent, remembered the feel of this particular body pressed against hers.

'Fern!' He was checking her all over now, his broad hands feeling her head, her face, roving over her chest.

'Are you breathing okay?'

Considering where his hand was at present, she was lucky she was breathing at all. She nodded and tried to croak out the words, *I'm okay*.

'Somebody call an ambulance!' he yelled over his shoulder, then kissed her fiercely on the forehead. 'Hang on, Fern. Hang on. I couldn't cope if…not when I've never…'

He stopped abruptly, probably because she was banging on his chest with the flat of her hand. He brushed the hair out of her eyes and tenderly held her face in his hands, a look of desperation in his eyes. 'What?' he whispered.

'You're squashing me.'

A look of horror crossed his face, almost comical in its intensity, and he sprang up to stand. 'Where's that ambulance?' he bellowed at no one in particular. Fern hauled herself to stand beside him.

'Josh! Will you stop? I'm fine. I'm breathing fine. I've been trying to tell you all along.'

He stared at her. 'You mean, you're not… you're…but you've eaten some of that sandwich.'

She stooped to pick up the now-flattened carton. 'Yes. Cheese and sun-dried tomato. I was about to throw the lettuce in the bin when I tripped over my own feet.'

'You…you didn't eat crayfish?' At the start of the sentence he was just bemused; by the end he was starting to look furious. He strode off towards the bin and looked inside it. Why, she didn't know, and she had a pretty good inkling that he didn't either. He stomped back towards her. He was angry with her about this? Seriously? He had no right. No right at all.

'Just how stupid do you think I am, Josh Adams? Do you really think I'm brainless enough to scoff down a crayfish sandwich only a day after I discover I've got a shellfish allergy?'

The look on his face told her everything she needed to know. Now he wasn't the only one who was head-thumping angry.

'You know what? I don't need a big brother. I don't need protecting. I wish you'd get that into your thick head,' she said, tapping the side of her skull with a finger. She needed more than that from him, more of everything from him, but she wasn't going to get it. It was darkly funny that Josh Adams seemed to have found a rut of his own now that she'd clambered out of hers.

'I'm off to get another sandwich before they

run out,' she yelled and stalked away. 'And you'd better do something about putting a stop to that ambulance.'

CHAPTER ELEVEN

JOSH held the camera steady and took a picture of the Thames looking back towards the city from the top of Tower Bridge.

'All done?'

He and Fern were speaking—just. Gone was the easy camaraderie, the near-telepathic exchange of ideas. In their place economical phrases and curt directions.

She was really angry with him, which wasn't fair at all. *She* hadn't been the one to get the shock of her life—for the second time in two days. *She* hadn't seen her whole life flash before her eyes and drain away. All she'd suffered was a squashed sandwich and she had no business to be giving him those superior, infuriatingly calm looks. He wasn't fooled for a second. He knew that underneath the calm façade her emotions were a boiling pot.

The sound of feet thumping on the walkway

between the two towers of the bridge caused them both to whirl round. Pat and Lily, a mother and daughter team, who *had* been three minutes behind them appeared. Instantly, Fern and Josh started running in the opposite direction. They'd had no sight of the front-runners yet, which was not good news, and they didn't need the next team catching them up.

After running down about a million steps—the sign on the wall said three hundred, but he didn't believe it for a second—they grabbed the next clue from a marshal and stood panting on the pavement to read it.

'Oh, blow! It's another of those cryptic ones.' He handed the card to Fern and she read it aloud.

'"*Start with citrus fruit and end with the bell of indecision.*" Is that it?' She shook her head. 'I really don't have the brain cells for this today. "Start with citrus fruit"? What does that mean?'

'A fruit market?'

They both frowned.

'You're right,' he said. 'We've done that already. It has to be something different.'

Fern started jogging northwards along the bridge, muttering *citrus fruit* over and over. 'What kind of citrus fruit?'

'Lemons? Limes? Oranges? Grapefruit?' he offered.

She skidded to a halt and he almost crashed into her. 'Say that again!'

'Grapefruit?'

'No. No…' She smiled at him, the first he'd seen all day. 'Before that. Oranges and lemons! It's like the old children's rhyme.'

A spike of excitement shot through him. 'Oranges and lemons said the bells of St Clements…'

Now she was jumping up and down. 'I bet it's a trail, like the tube stations were. We have to visit each of the churches from the rhyme in turn and take a picture.'

He held out a hand and she slapped the map into his waiting palm. 'Now, where the heck is St Clement's Church?'

Fern was already leafing through their well-thumbed guidebook. 'What about the others?' She mumbled the rhyme out loud. '"Oranges and lemons" say the bells of St Clement's. "You owe me five farthings" say the bells of St Martin's… Oh, crumbs! I can't remember the rest.'

'"When will you pay me?"' he was shouting now. The magic was back, the zinging, idea-bouncing magic was back. 'Say the bells of…' He racked his brain. It was on the tip of his tongue.

'Old Bailey,' she finished. 'We can work out the rest on the way.'

Inwardly, he sighed. Perhaps the proverbs were wrong. Perhaps you *could* go back. Perhaps he could return to a time when he hadn't lost her friendship for ever.

Clever, thought Fern, as they stood on the other side of the road from St Mary-le-Bow. The bell of indecision. The last line of the nursery rhyme chimed in her head. Not yes, not no, but somewhere in between. *'I do not know' say the great bells of Bow.*

Josh put the camera back in his pocket. 'What now? Where next?'

She looked around. 'There has to be a marshal close, or a clue somewhere. Why don't we go inside?'

Just inside the front entrance was a box on a stand with a Secret London logo on it. She reached inside and pulled out an envelope and handed it to Josh. Quickly, mouthing the numbers as she went, she counted off the remaining envelopes.

Nine. The realisation made her giddy.

'Josh! We're first here. We could win this, we really could.'

He showed her the clue. *Full circle. Back to the beginning wiser…and possibly richer.*

'Trafalgar Square,' they both said at the same time, just as Kate and Aidan ran into the church entrance, heard what they said and set off running again. Every muscle in her body leapt into action. As one, she and Josh gave chase.

'Nearest tube station?' she yelled at Josh as she struggled with the map. It was flapping in her face and seriously slowing her down.

'Canon Street?' he yelled back, a little too loudly. Kate and Aidan, who were breaking away, nodded at each other, pointed at a sign for Canon Street and sprinted off.

'Me and my big mouth,' Josh muttered and picked up speed.

She grabbed on to his backpack to stop him and waved the map at him. 'Don't sweat it. Canon Street tube is closed on Sundays and Mansion House is closer, anyway. You might have accidentally given us our lead back.'

The tube was virtually empty—not surprising for a Sunday morning in the financial and business heart of the city. Even though there were seats available, she and Josh stood either side of a set of double doors, their backs pressed against the perspex carriage dividers.

After the sprint to the station they had a few minutes of enforced stillness before the doors hissed open and the madness began again.

The bubbling rage that had consumed her at breakfast time had dissipated and her mind was now as clear as a mill pond. Josh had said categorically that he didn't feel *that way* about her, but his reaction this morning proved him a liar. The truth was he cared more than he wanted to.

All her wishes had been used up, or so she'd thought. Maybe she had one last chance in the silence of this tube ride. When the race ended she just knew that Josh would run again and she might never pin him down.

The doors opened and a handful of people flowed on to the train. She couldn't tell how many because she was too busy looking at him. As if he sensed her gaze on him, he looked up and their eyes locked. Her heart skipped and stuttered in her chest. There was something there. *Something* in his eyes. She couldn't look away.

The doors closed and the train rumbled away

from the station. She took a deep breath and held it. The next stop was theirs. It was now or never and, if there was one thing she'd learned from Josh this week, it was that she should grab chances when they presented themselves.

Her eyes were full of unspoken words—syllables and sounds he shouldn't want to hear. With that defiant yet vulnerable look on her face she was so beautiful. Time had stopped and they were here alone in their own separate bubble, hurtling towards an unknown destination. For the first time in his life he wasn't sure if he was feeling all that adventurous.

The lights flickered and the train started to slow. If anything, the look in her eyes grew even fiercer. He was pinned by her gaze.

The train was moving so slowly now it had virtually come to a stop. She raised her chin, opened her mouth and only then did the words that had been flashing in her eyes hit his eardrums as sound waves.

'I love you.'

And then the doors opened and she was running. It took him a full second to realise that he was supposed to be doing the same.

He hardly noticed the interior of the tube station as he ran through it, or the busy, narrow street that led up on to the Strand. He dodged taxis and reversing delivery vans on autopilot.

She loved him.

Inside he was flying—the best rush he'd ever had powered his legs as he chased her up the hill and on to the busy main road. His instincts should really be telling him to sprint in the opposite direction but, somehow, all he could do was run *to* her.

A sudden realisation hit him with such force that it stopped him in his tracks.

He loved her too.

A horn screamed at him and he jumped back on to the kerb. The noise of the city, the sirens, the crunching gears, church bells and people flooded back into his consciousness. He woke up.

Fern had just about reached the other side of the road after having sprinted straight across, but the lights had just changed and now the stream of buses, taxis and cars was too busy to negotiate.

She turned, a look of sheer panic on her face. 'Josh!'

That was when he saw them—Kate and Aidan—appear from nowhere further up the square and race across a clear stretch of road. They must have been right behind them all the time. Suddenly it didn't matter how many damn buses there were. He weaved in and out, ignoring the shouts and honkings.

The stage and finishing post were clearly visible at the base of Nelson's Column now. Fern started running before he reached her, her face pink with exertion. He dodged one last taxi, caught her up and grabbed her hand. Together they gave everything they had in an attempt to reach the Secret London flag first.

A crowd had gathered, cheering and yelling, making it hard to work out where Kate and Aidan were. It wasn't until they were within metres of the finish that he realised both teams were neck and neck.

Everything went into slow motion. The shouts of the crowd boomed in his ears and he felt a great weight tugging him down. Fern had stumbled and her heavy backpack caused her to crash on to the ground, taking him with her. Instinctively, he clutched at her and pulled her to him so at least he partially broke her fall.

The crowd went wild and he knew without

raising himself on his grazed and bleeding palms that Kate and Aidan had crossed the finish line.

They sat on the edge of one of the fountains and he watched Fern inspect the dressing on her lacerated knee. Neither of them had spoken in the last ten minutes. They'd just picked themselves up, smiled for the cameras and numbly allowed the St John's Ambulance crew to patch them up.

Josh closed his eyes and tried not to let the sense of defeat engulf him.

'I'm sorry,' he said.

She looked nervously at him. 'About what?'

As usual she was being far too nice. 'About losing the race. If I'd crossed that road with you we'd have made it.' He shook his head. 'A split-second, a missed chance. That was all it took. I should have gone when you did.'

But he'd been too busy reeling from her revelation to pay attention.

'Don't be daft. We might have beaten them still if I hadn't tripped over my own feet again. What a pair of losers we are!' She let out a broken laugh and it ended in a sigh. 'I know it's a cliché to say that it was the taking part that was important, but it really was. I learned things about a city that I thought I knew so well and—' she drew her knees up and rested her chin on her good one '—I learned a lot about myself, about what's important in life.'

He nodded. He'd certainly learned something over the last few days. The problem was that it was all spinning round inside his head at the moment and he hadn't had a chance to work out what that might be.

'I meant what I said.' She tipped her head to look at him. 'I do love you.'

He swallowed.

'Tell me you don't feel the same way.'

He returned her gaze as openly and honestly as he could. The fact that he'd been stupid enough to fall for her wouldn't change the outcome if they got together. 'I can't.' He wouldn't lie to her, but he couldn't give her the happy ending she'd been wishing for either. They were grown-ups and they needed to face reality.

She slid off the wall and on to her feet, a fierce, brave expression on her face. Her head moved gently from side to side. 'You coward.'

'No.' That wasn't it at all. He was no good at the emotional stuff, no good at anything permanent.

'I always thought you were so brave. I idolised you,' she said quietly, staring across the packed square. 'I thought you did all those exciting things, went to those exciting places, because you weren't afraid of anything.'

So had he. Why then, was this conversation making the blood race in his ears and his stomach churn?

'I should have realised it sooner.' She was almost talking to herself. 'You started running when Ryan died—running from all those overwhelming feelings you didn't want to face—and you've never stopped. For crying out loud, you didn't even go to his funeral!'

She was right. He hadn't been able to do it. 'I couldn't face it. It was…' Even those words were too hard.

Her face softened and it looked as if she'd reached some kind of decision. 'You've never properly grieved for Ryan, and you need to. Until you do, you're never going to be ready for a grown-up relationship. You have to start living, feeling again—*all* the experiences, not just the good ones, so intense they blot out everything else.' She sighed. 'When you let people close, when you love people—' the soft tenderness in her eyes broke his heart '—it gets difficult and painful and complicated sometimes. That's the nature of human relationships.'

She moved closer and her voice was almost a whisper. 'Love can be exhilarating and terrifying and wonderful—all the things you used to say you wanted out of life.'

Slowly, she raised her hand to trace the skin of his cheek. He closed his eyes. It was too hard to look at her. Too hard to watch her heart breaking in front of him. Her lips brushed his and she kissed him—sweetly, softly, slowly—then stood back.

'Goodbye, Josh.'

His automatic reaction was to reach for her and he caught her wrist in his hand. She shook her head and the tears started to flow.

'You were right after all.' Her lips pressed together, then wobbled. 'And little sisters hate it when their honorary big brothers do that.' She made an attempt at a soggy smile and slid her hand out of his grasp.

'Fern…'

'We don't have a future together. Not unless you sort this out.' She stepped backwards. 'For my whole life I've waited for you to say *yes* to me, but now I'm saying *no* to you. I'm going to start living instead of hiding.' And with that she backed away and melted into the crowd.

He should have known there'd be fresh flowers. He reached down to the bouquet sitting directly in front of the headstone and turned the card over.

The bunch of riotous summer flowers was from Fern. The simple message read: *Here goes! All my love, Fern.*

He dropped the card and took a few steps backwards. He hadn't seen her in three weeks. And he'd been telling himself he was fine with that. His feet were like lead weights as he stepped forward again and put the sad-looking bunch of carnations he'd found at a petrol station next to her bouquet.

He had a plane to catch in six hours. Visiting Ryan's grave hadn't been an afterthought, more like something he'd been avoiding. In the end he'd made up his mind just to go and do it quickly, spur of the moment. It hadn't made it any easier.

His mobile phone buzzed in his pocket and he ignored it. It would be Callum, his business partner, fussing about the last-minute details of his trip. Today he was off on a fact-finding trip to Cambodia. Next year they were hoping to offer an 'explore the temples of Angkor Wat' expedition. And once he'd finished with that he planned to find a beach in Thailand and lie on it for a whole month.

It was time to move on. Mum and Dad were in Scotland. The grapevine must have been working wonderfully because when he'd arrived home, dressings on his hands and a grim don't-even-try-talking-to-me look on his face, they'd backed off and given him space. And when he'd insisted on paying for their trip they'd just nodded.

He didn't think he'd ever had to endure anyone's pity before. It was horrendous. And he had nowhere near the grace Fern had to smile politely and pretend he wasn't gutted. He had a lot to learn from her.

Eventually, he'd worked out what he'd learned from the treasure hunt too. He'd learnt that he could miss opportunities, even though he'd thought he was immune to that. And he'd learnt that he'd been blind to the treasure in his life until it had disappeared.

He missed Fern.

He'd looked up her address and had thought

about going to see her, but once again he'd waited too long. She'd gone away. And, anyway, there was no point. The words she'd said when she'd left him in Trafalgar Square mocked him. He wasn't any further on now than he had been then. He wasn't ready for her and he certainly didn't deserve her.

He pictured the terror on her face the day she'd stood on top of the crane waiting to do the bungee jump and thrust his fists into his jacket pockets, disgusted with himself. She was right. He was a coward.

He looked at Ryan's grave. He couldn't stay here any more. It wasn't doing any good. He didn't *feel* anything. Pebbled paths criss-crossed St Mark's churchyard and he just picked one and followed it.

All his noble spoutings about not wanting to ruin their friendship, not wanting to hurt their parents, had been excuses, just as she'd said. He'd got his wish. He'd backed off and left her heart alone—although he was probably kidding himself if he believed it was undamaged—and still their friendship was in tatters. Thinking it could have returned to normal had just been a fantasy.

What he'd feared had happened anyway. And,

try as he might to leave those messy feelings behind when he got on the plane this evening, he suspected they'd be his travelling companions; their barbs dug in far too deep to be shaken off easily.

He sighed, realising that he'd come full circle, and was standing back in front of Ryan's grave.

Even if he wanted to, he couldn't see Fern now. Helen Chambers had told his mother that her daughter had gone away to France. He'd been left behind, as he'd deserved to be. She'd been brave enough to take a leap of faith when he had only run for cover. Gutless, that was what he was.

The yellow carnations looked shabby on their own. Ryan deserved more than that. He ripped the soggy paper off them and started poking the stems in between the sunflowers and greenery of Fern's bouquet. When he'd finished he stood back and looked at his haphazard work. Ryan would have laughed his head off.

Just that one thought squeezed his heart so hard that moisture popped out of one eye. Until today he'd been too scared to come to this spot, but now he was here, he knew he couldn't leave. Not until he'd said some long-overdue things to his best friend.

His backside hit the dewy grass with a thud and he bowed over his crossed legs.

'Sorry, mate…' his voice was raw '…I let you down…and I let her down…'

And he put his head in his hands and began to cry.

Fern's mobile rang and, as it had done so many times in the last few weeks, her pulse hiccupped. It's not him, she told herself crossly.

The display told her it was her mother and she was tempted to pretend she hadn't seen it, but that would sentence her to a morning of panic calls every five minutes just to check she was okay, which would seriously suck all the fun out of the sightseeing she had planned. She slid her phone open with a sigh.

'Hello, Mum.'

'Hello, darling. What are you up to?'

She should have been used to her mother's nervous checking of her whereabouts by now but, to be honest, at twenty-eight she was thoroughly sick and tired of it. She wanted to say, *I've decided to strip off and become a cancan dancer at the Moulin Rouge.* What she actually said was, 'Well, I'm standing outside the Louvre right now and, after I've wandered round and had some lunch, I'm going to the Eiffel Tower.'

'Silence for a few seconds. 'Isn't that awfully high up?'

'Mum, honestly! They have health and safety procedures here in France too, you know. I'm not going to fall off.'

'Well, just you be careful.'

I always am, she thought. Too careful.

'What sort of time will you be at the Eiffel Tower?'

This was a new level of monitoring, even for Mum. She'd been absolutely awful since she'd found out about the bungee jump. Fern rolled her eyes. 'Why do you want to know?'

Her mother coughed. 'Just…well, just because I like to know where you are when you're away from home.'

Oh, for goodness' sake! The information would have to be provided or the interrogation could last for hours. 'I'm aiming to get there about two o'clock. Satisfied?'

Her mother sounded very pleased with herself. 'That's lovely, darling. Have a nice time. And don't forget to call us if you have any news, okay?'

'Bye, Mum. Give my love to Dad.'

Fern closed her phone and returned it to her bag, frowning. News? That would be a laugh. She was just a single girl spending a week in Paris. It was hardly headline stuff.

Getting away had just seemed like a good idea. She could understand why Josh was inclined to do it now. A different place, new tastes and experiences. She'd hoped it would help her get everything into perspective.

She made her way into the Louvre, deliciously cool after the baking July sun, and drifted from room to room. The trip had been part of her 'moving up and moving on' strategy. After losing the race, she'd felt so awful about depriving the Leukaemia Research Trust of the prize money that she'd emptied her savings account—her nest egg, her security—and had given five thousand pounds to the appeal out of her own money. There'd been just enough left to splash out.

New horizons.

She stood still and acknowledged the familiar wilting feeling she got every time she thought about 'moving on'. For so long she'd waited for Josh, but now the waiting was over.

Right now, she couldn't ever imagine erasing him from her heart. She still burst into tears at the oddest of times, but she was allowing herself to grieve for both him and the death of long-cherished dreams. When the process was complete she'd be free to find love with someone else in the future. Now she was open to it; her heart was no longer barricaded. Josh had done that much for her, at least.

Eventually she found herself standing in front of the *Mona Lisa*. That smile really was unbearably smug. She put her hands on her hips and raised her eyebrows.

You look pretty pleased with yourself, sitting there all happy and content. What's your secret? she silently asked. *What do you know that I don't?*

Josh fastened his seat belt and stared out of the aeroplane window. Even the first class seat didn't feel comfortable on this trip.

He liked to sit near the window, to see all the different scenery, exciting places he yet had to visit, as he flew high above. His destination today was somewhere new and exciting. Somewhere he'd wanted to visit for years. He should be pumped, but actually his heart was feeling a little sore and bruised.

The aeroplane taxied to the end of the runway

and, as the jet engine shook with restrained fierceness and the scenery started to roll by faster and faster, his thoughts echoed the message on the bouquet on Ryan's grave.

Here goes.

A slight haze blurred the edges of the horizon. Fern peered through the wide wire mesh that stopped her plummeting to her death. It was beautiful up here, still and peaceful. She could see the Arc de Triomphe, cars chasing round it like frenzied insects, and the Seine, gleaming regally as it curved through this beautiful, romantic city.

A great, heavy breath left her. She didn't want to be here alone. But she was. And she had to deal with it. Her fingers curled against the wire in front of her and she rested her head against it while she braced herself for the torrent of emotions that surged through her. She rode the wave and felt herself calm again, pleased she hadn't let the tears fall this time.

A prickling sensation on the back of her neck made her go still. One by one, every fine hair stood to attention. The noise of the city dwindled. A pair of warm, steady hands circled her waist. The skin there, sensitive even through the fabric of her T-shirt, tingled and sang. Electricity leapt through her, zapping her from head to toe as he leaned in close enough for her to feel the beat of his heart against her back.

He was in paradise—white sand, crystal-blue sea, palm trees swaying gently in the tropical breeze. Josh stared across the beach at the small group of people who had followed him here for this latest adventure. His hands were shaking, but the others didn't seem nervous at all.

But they had no idea how wonderful, amazing and totally terrifying the next hour would be. No idea at all. He took a deep breath and turned to look up the beach.

Any moment now it would start. A sudden and unexpected burst of adrenaline flooded through him. A primal fight or flight response, but he refused to move. This time he was staying put.

A flutter in the breeze, a whisper of voices, the way the crowd around him went still and turned, told him it was time. His heart rate rocketed.

Ryan, mate, I hope you're looking down on me

and smiling. I'm keeping my promise the best way I know how.

And, with the knowledge that deep down to his toes he had made the right decision, he turned around also.

She was gorgeous, stunning, everything he could have fantasised about and more. Her golden hair wasn't swept up and tidy, but tumbling in loose waves around her shoulders, a single over-sized hibiscus bloom above one ear.

The dress was simple—white, long—any more than that he didn't register, only the fact that the soft layers fluttered around her legs, tickling the tops of her bare feet. He started to smile, so wide his face muscles hurt. This truly was the biggest rush of his life, standing here, watching Fern walk towards him, a sweet smile on her lips and the blaze of love for him in her eyes.

He had been the stupidest man on the planet. Truly. Thankfully, she'd agreed to make him the luckiest.

Hardly aware that music had been playing while she'd walked down the beach towards him, he only noticed it now as the last strains died away. She handed her bouquet to the bridesmaid and he took her hands in his, not caring if it wasn't the proper time yet, and they turned to face the minister.

The simple service started immediately. Neither of them had wanted anything long and drawn-out; they'd waited too long for this moment already. She smiled cheekily as he promised to love, comfort and *protect* her, but it was okay because a few seconds later she promised to do exactly the same for him.

Then it was time to taste her sweet lips, although it was a little short for his liking, and walk back up the beach together, joined for always.

As the wedding reception got underway, he drew her into a quiet corner and kissed the band of gold on her left hand. 'Inside here there's another promise. An inscription.'

Fern's eyes widened. He hadn't said anything! This was typical Josh. Every day was a surprise with this incredible man. Better than anything she could ever have dreamed up. 'Inside the ring? I didn't see it.'

He grinned at her. 'Always read the small print, remember?'

She whacked him on the arm for being cheeky. 'It all happened so quickly I didn't have a chance to see and I don't want to take it off now.' She twiddled it on her finger. 'What does it say?'

He sobered. 'In my heart for eternity.'

She felt her eyes go misty. 'That's beautiful. I'm in your heart from this day forward.'

'No.' He took her face in his hands and kissed her.

'No?' she breathed against his lips.

'Eternity means past and present too, not just the future. It was always you, Fern. You were always in my heart; I just wasn't brave enough to admit it.'

She didn't care if people were watching, she pulled him to her and kissed him in a way that left him in no doubt as to how lucky he was going to get later that night.

Only Josh swung her into his arms and headed for the honeymoon suite a little earlier than planned. 'They'll understand,' he whispered into her ear. And from the cheers and whistles she could hear as they left the room, she reckoned they just might. 'Save us some cake!' he yelled over his shoulder.

And, as he laid her gently down on the vast white bed, he smiled that sexy smile that always did crazy things to her insides. 'So, Mrs Adams, are you ready to embark on the biggest adventure of our lives?'

She threw her head back and laughed before pulling him down on top of her. There was only one thing she could say to that, wasn't there?

'Yes.'

MILLS & BOON PUBLISH EIGHT LARGE PRINT TITLES A MONTH. THESE ARE THE EIGHT TITLES FOR OCTOBER 2008.

THE SHEIKH'S BLACKMAILED MISTRESS
Penny Jordan

THE MILLIONAIRE'S INEXPERIENCED LOVE-SLAVE
Miranda Lee

BOUGHT: THE GREEK'S INNOCENT VIRGIN
Sarah Morgan

BEDDED AT THE BILLIONAIRE'S CONVENIENCE
Cathy Williams

THE PREGNANCY PROMISE
Barbara McMahon

THE ITALIAN'S CINDERELLA BRIDE
Lucy Gordon

SAYING YES TO THE MILLIONAIRE
Fiona Harper

HER ROYAL WEDDING WISH
Cara Colter

0908 Rom LP